T0054189

HER BLOOD'S
WARNING

HER BLOOD'S
WARNING

KYMBERLEY COOK

TATE PUBLISHING
AND ENTERPRISES, LLC

Her Blood's Warning
Copyright © 2012 by Kymberley Cook. All rights reserved.

No part of this publication may be reproduced, stored in a retrieval system or transmitted in any way by any means, electronic, mechanical, photocopy, recording or otherwise without the prior permission of the author except as provided by USA copyright law.

This novel is a work of fiction. Names, descriptions, entities, and incidents included in the story are products of the author's imagination. Any resemblance to actual persons, events, and entities is entirely coincidental.

The opinions expressed by the author are not necessarily those of Tate Publishing, LLC.

Published by Tate Publishing & Enterprises, LLC
127 E. Trade Center Terrace | Mustang, Oklahoma 73064 USA
1.888.361.9473 | www.tatepublishing.com

Tate Publishing is committed to excellence in the publishing industry. The company reflects the philosophy established by the founders, based on Psalm 68:11,
"The Lord gave the word and great was the company of those who published it."

Book design copyright © 2012 by Tate Publishing, LLC. All rights reserved.
Cover design by Joel Uber
Interior design by Chelsea Womble

Published in the United States of America

ISBN: 978-1-62024-645-0
1. Fiction / Fantasy / Contemporary
2. Fiction / Romance / Fantasy
12.06.11

ACKNOWLEDGMENTS

For my husband, Shane, thank you for listening to all my stories and inspiring me.

To my editors, Iris Shepard and Laura Morgan, I enjoyed working with you both on this novel, and your invaluable suggestions were greatly appreciated.

THE MESSAGE

1972

I had spent the last two decades on holiday in Europe, sheltering in the ruins of old castles lining the jagged coasts of the North Sea. I needed no fire to keep me warm, and I covered my tracks well. The Europeans had no idea I had been living among them.

It was easy to feed here, just as anywhere else in the world. I needed to drink human's blood to survive, but blood's scent never aroused my hunger. It was a criminal's corrupted aura that ignited my thirst. Europe had its fair share of villains. No one missed the killers, thieves, and rapists that I lured away from cities into the forests, mountains, or abandoned shacks to kill. Our vampiric code asserted we only feed on the most decadent of characters. I enticed these vile humans with the promise of money, women, or drugs, giving them a time and place to meet for the goods. I never experienced the anguish of going hungry because one didn't show.

I listened and watched for ghosts from those who had fallen, either in battle or from the plague. I was lonely, and I would have preferred the company of ghosts over humans. A ghost was already dead; I did not have to worry about desiring to kill it or its death weighing on my conscience. I was often tortured by the thoughts of my victims.

I often thought about a beautiful woman I slew. I noticed her from a great distance as I scouted Paris on a night long ago. I had no intentions of killing her until she turned to look at me, revealing her nature. She had killed several young children at an orphanage she ran while selling many others into slavery. Instead of luring her from the city, I pulled her into a dark alley, covered her mouth so she could not scream, and drank quickly. When I was full, I ran to sea and dove in to wash the bloodstains from my body. Only later did the anguish settle in. The same questions always came to my mind when I thought of her: What had caused her to become a monster? Was it the way she had been raised, or was she evil upon birth? It was harder for me to attack a woman. Killing her would always weigh on my conscience. I expected her to haunt me out of revenge, but she hadn't.

I discovered nothing out of the ordinary. There were no ghosts, except for the imaginary ones lingering in my memory. Disappointed but having nothing better to do, I stayed in Europe longer than I had originally planned.

One night, I traveled across the Netherlands in great haste. Every so often while scouting for food, I entered the city of Den Haag in the province of South Holland to check for news from home. I knew a portly vampire with a sparse halo of hair by the name of John Newman who lived in the city. He was quite old but hadn't aged beyond his early forties. He had been born during the reign of Queen Elizabeth I, and even though I didn't care much for his character, I once enjoyed hearing history from his point of view—the stories not recorded in any book.

John Newman was no friend of mine, but I used him for receiving and holding my messages. I really only had one vampire friend who currently knew how to contact me and would write to me on a semiregular basis. I did not want to get acquainted with others like myself. I was reclusive when I was human, and it had not changed, but the loneliness would eventually creep back into my conscience and nag until I addressed it. During those times, I needed my friend.

It had been six months since I had last dropped by John's, and I was not looking forward to this visit because John not only fed upon criminals but also the sick and dying, homeless stragglers, and poor. He felt he was doing them a favor by ending their pain. I had tried to kindly explain why it was wrong to kill humans in these conditions and that the Ragnvaldr, our council, would not like it. I could not sway him, so we decided not to discuss the matter. He viewed my morals as rigid and conservative. Through the centuries, he had become wicked and no longer deserved his vampire powers. He was no different than the humans I hunted. I thirsted for his blood upon each and every uncomfortable visit. I knew killing him would hold a consequence from the Ragnvaldr, so I suppressed my urge.

I stood knocking at his cottage door during a hard, cold rain. "Got anything for me?"

John opened the door, excited by my sudden visit. "More stories, if you wish, Thadacus."

"Not in the mood. I can see you have had company," I said politely, yet I was deeply disgusted. The odor of his kill was still present in his mouth.

"Not company—dinner. The old woman was stricken with pneumonia and drenched from the downpour. She will be taken out back and buried. She won't suffer anymore. I felt sorry for her. I was showing her kindness with the promise of a warm fire and hot soup."

I imagined a feeble, old woman trusting the filthy beast to feed her and then pleading for her life in her last moments. It was not his place to decide that she had lived long enough. I wanted to punish him.

"Did you provide her with soup and warmth?" I asked.

"No. Why prolong her misery? Come in, will you? I haven't told you everything I know about the tyrant Henry VIII."

You are the tyrant, I thought, declining the offer. I wondered if the old woman had a family. Were they searching for her right now?

"I best go. I am headed for France tomorrow."

"You have already been there, have you not?"

"Yes, but it has been five years since my last visit, and I grow tired of the coast. I should let you get back to your business."

"Too bad. I do enjoy your company."

I turned to walk off. On many nights I would stand or run naked through the rain, but on my trips to town, I wore clothes. My jeans and shirt were weighted down and clinging to my body. I was uncomfortable and wanted to rid myself of them and John.

"Wait! You do have a letter. I believe it is from your old friend... What is his name? Oh, yes. Egan Braun! I can always tell his letters apart from all the others. He is one of the few who still uses wax and ring to seal his messages."

"He is the only one who writes me."

"Right," he said slowly. "Well, I knew it could not possibly be a woman. With your ethics, a nun would not be good enough for you."

I nodded with a slight smile, even though I was highly irritated.

"Do not worry. The seal is not broken," he joked, but I had no sense of humor.

He came back, sniffing the paper with his bulbous nose. "Louisiana has a different smell. I must visit there sometime."

Great. That's all I need. It's annoying enough knowing you're here in Europe, I thought, taking my letter from his hand.

"Do come back. Like I said, Henry VIII..."

I nodded to humor him then was gone into the downpour before he could say another word.

By the time I reached the outskirts of the city, the rain had been replaced by thick fog. I stopped at a lamppost and opened my letter. Egan had requested that I return to America. He needed me. After reading it, my plans suddenly changed. I did not know if Egan had good or bad news, and I was worried about my friend.

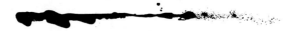

The next night I spent several hours running full speed along the coast until I reached the city of Le Havre. It was practically a straight line between the two towns, and I knew the way well. Once I had arrived, I bought a new pair of jeans, a black cotton shirt, and a hotel room. That was easy enough; I kept money stashed in different places for the sole purpose of traveling. I unbuttoned my jeans and pulled them off my legs. After showering and washing my grimy black hair, I placed the Do Not Disturb sign up and closed all the drapes. A maid ignored it and came in anyway. Her aura was not the dark violet that indicated a human was consumed with pure evil; hers was a medium lavender, so I assumed she was a petty thief, stealing for the rush of it all. I was hungry, but now was not the time. I had to wait.

"What are you doing in here?" I asked coldly. "Can you not read?"

Driven by thirst, my fangs shoved my lips back.

"Sorry. I did not see the sign. I will return at a more convenient time," apologized the maid, startled anyone was in the room. She had knocked beforehand, but I had not responded.

"If you know what's good for you, you will not return," I warned. Had she seen my unnatural eyes or fangs? I thought about tracking her, but I decided not to. I knew I would regret it afterward.

At dusk the next day, I boarded an airplane and flew to my home country, America. The flight was smooth, but I had to force myself to sit back and appear like I did not mind being trapped inside a fuselage. I hated handing that piece of my journey over to the pilot; I wanted to be the one in control. I often dreamed of flying like a bat or bird, but sadly that part of the vampire's myth did not hold any truth.

The airport in Tulsa was crowded, and I wasn't ready to be around people. I had no tolerance for small talk, cigarette smoke, rude pedestrians packing the sidewalks, misbehaving children, and I didn't trust myself around them. I sensed the desire to do wrong in more of them than not, which elevated my hunger.

Many humans of the modern world did not appreciate their lives or the time that had been given to them. So many squandered away their days by doing drugs and shrinking from their responsibilities as parents. They did not know right from wrong, so they could not teach it. I pitied this class of humans until they killed or raped without mercy, and then I had no problem eradicating them.

Once I reached the outskirts of the city, I instructed the cab driver to let me out. I would walk or run the rest of my journey.

"Here?" the cabbie asked stunned. "Man, you could get mugged. This is not a good spot. I can drive you a little farther at no cost if money is an issue. At least let me get you to a gas station."

"Thank you for your kindness, but I will be fine," I said, handing him a wad of cash for his rare generosity.

It was early summer, which was not my favorite season. I no longer grew sweaty, short of breath, or sunburned, but I could not let go of such human memories so easily; I felt like I should still suffer from the sun's heat. However, summer also brought with it certain things I enjoyed, like the sound of frogs croaking and a slight breeze carrying the smell of grass covered by night's first touch of dew.

I could not run at lightning speed, but once I got going, my bones, which were not affected by the shocks of gravity, allowed me to sprint into almost a blur. I traveled at that rate southeastward toward Louisiana so Egan would not have to wait, but I had chosen the airport in Tulsa for a reason. I desired to revisit the foothills of the Ozark Mountains. It had been a century since I had journeyed that way. I remembered the landscape with hills coated in trees so thick and green that bare spots were not visible and fields colored deep gold by thick grasses. Barns made with rusted, tin roofs and aged gray wood dotted the countryside. Numerous rivers and creeks cut through the valleys. Some streams flowed down jagged bluffs into hidden cascades. It was about a fifty-mile detour, but Egan would never suspect I had dallied for a couple hours.

Something made me stop in a pasture near a small farm-house in the rural town of Prairie Grove, Arkansas. I didn't need to rest. My kind, we do not get tired.

Fireflies—it was fireflies that made me stop. I had never seen so many gathered in a field at one time. There must have been three to four fireflies on each stalk of grass while many more hovered slightly above, signaling their mates. Their name suited them, *fire*, but this was an enjoyable fire, one without suffocating smoke and heat. The air was cool, and for a moment I felt alive and magical. I suddenly wished I had a mate, one that could revel in the moment with me. I wanted to share my feelings.

A screen door slammed.

I quickly ducked and parted the sage grass so I could see who was coming. I watched and listened; I was hungry.

"Oh, Richard, I told you. Isn't it breathtaking?" said a young woman, holding the hand of a small, pale child with ginger-colored curls. She could not have been a little more than year old.

"Bhren, I have never seen so many. It looks like our cow pasture has caught on fire. Mom! Dad! Come out here and take a look at this!" yelled Richard.

Soon an old couple stepped outside and watched the spectacle.

I suppressed the growing cube of ice within my gut—my hunger. I would have to wait to feed.

"Interesting… Well, I am ready for bed," said the elderly man, walking back inside. For a moment, I imagined draining him while his blood warmed my stomach. I gasped and shivered as I pushed the sinful thought from my mind.

"I'm right behind you," said the elderly woman, quickly following.

"Rhymee, stand still!" said Bhren, but the little girl pulled free of her mother's grip.

The child watched the fireflies for a moment then seemed to do a dance in their honor.

"Rhymee, come here, or you're going in!" sternly warned the mother.

"Bhren, let her have a moment. She has been cooped up all day," said Richard. I assumed he was Rhymee's father.

The mother tapped her foot for a moment then sighed.

"I suppose you're right," she said, standing even closer to her husband.

"I don't know which is more beautiful, the fireflies or the moon," he said. "It seems closer to us tonight."

Bhren nodded in quiet agreement then kissed her husband on the cheek. They quickly became distracted by each other.

I was just about to continue on my journey when the little one turned and walked toward the field in which I was hiding.

She finally stood perfectly still and seemed to stare through the darkness. I didn't move, except to lower my eyelids to slits so she wouldn't see my reflective retinas.

"See the moon?" she asked.

There was no other being, not even animal, anywhere near me. My senses raced. Had she discovered me?

"Richard, she said her first sentence," said Bhren, running after the child and grabbing her excitedly. "Let's go tell Grandma what you said."

"Say it again!" said Richard enthusiastically, not believing his little girl had said so much at once.

Rhymee gazed in my direction longingly then at the moon, all the while struggling to free herself yet again from her mother's grip.

"See the moon! See the moon!" she yelled in my direction. She did not want to go back inside.

I laid down flat, smashing sage grass, baffled by what I had just witnessed, and for a while I gazed at the moon, trying to figure out what was so special about it on that night. Was the little girl gifted with supernatural powers? She was not vampire, but she was not ordinary. I could hear the blood flowing through her veins; she was human. Was it the moon or the fireflies mesmerizing me, or her? Her aura glowed with pure innocence, yet I sensed uncompromising strength. I had never felt anything like it. I wanted to shield her against all harm. I should not have allowed myself to feel her soul because I was from then on connected to it. I meditated for a while so I could muster the strength to continue south.

I stopped at a rest area and finally had a meal. The man in the long black trench coat was up to no good. I found a braided rope about three feet in length in his pocket. He had no ID or any other possessions. I guess he had planned on hitching a ride and had no certain destination in mind. His intentions were foul; he liked strangling his victims from the back seat.

Not much had changed since I had last visited Hammond, Louisiana. The strong aroma of honeysuckle overwhelmed my nostrils right after crossing the state line. The rest of my journey was uneventful.

A couple hours later, I arrived at Egan's. His residence wasn't much to look at from the outside. His house was two stories with white pillars and cement siding trimmed in black. There was very little grass in the yard. It seemed to grow only in patches. I supposed the soil was too acidic. Oddly, the house seemed to blend through the ages. Like a classic piece of clothing, it never completely fell out of style.

The front door was a deliberate eyesore. It was made of iron six inches thick with a gargoyle head for a knocker, and the windows were all barred. Most knew upon entering this house they would be trapped. I had laughed at salesmen pulling up in the circle drive as I watched from an upstairs window. They would step out of their vehicles, stare at the house for a moment, scratch their chins, and then they would get back in their cars and drive away quickly.

Inside the house was something different. Ancient mahogany floors were in all the rooms, except for the kitchen, which was laid with Egyptian stone. Intricately carved wood and gold trim lined all the ceilings and floors.

My friend was a collector of ancient artifacts and furniture. Marble statues from the Greeks were stuck in the corners here and there. He even had a throne from the ancient Scottish kings in his library; it was his favorite place to sit and read.

Before I could reach the door, it screeched open. "I sensed your presence. Come in, my friend." He gestured with welcoming arms.

My friend had been in his early sixties when he had been turned over a thousand years ago. I thought it was a true test and an amazing feat of his strength for him to live to an old age because during that period of time many humans died of disease or were killed in warfare. His hair was silver, yet he was still young in the face with very few wrinkles, and he was quite athletic.

"It is good to see you. How was England?" he asked in his hearty voice.

I sighed.

"That good, hey?"

"What news? Why am I needed?" I asked, seeming impatient but not meaning to.

"It is a long story. I will get to that, but first follow me. I have a gift for you," he said, sounding as if he already knew I would love it.

I quickly followed him up the stairs to the library, eager to know why he had sent for me, but in the back of my mind, I could not quit thinking of Rhymee.

THE OLD ONE'S DECISION

Egan walked over to his desk and picked up a leather-bound book and handed it carefully to me. "For you."

I could tell it was ancient by its brown pages and warped, worn cover.

"Grengham Seakirk did not part with this lightly, you know! It has been in Seakirk's possession for ages. I visited him years ago and was allowed to read it, but he supervised me the entire time. Talk about annoying! I have since enjoyed it in the comfort of my chair—alone."

"What is it about?" I asked curiously, almost too scared to open it, worried I would damage its delicate pages.

"It is a diary from a human who lived in the sixteenth century. He was from, I guess, what we would consider the upper class from that time period. I won't say more, except, enjoy," he said with a grin.

"Why, Egan? Why such an elaborate gift? I appreciate this beyond words, but I do not deserve it."

"You have been a good friend, and I have never had the pleasure of giving you anything," he responded sadly.

I stared at him in confusion, thinking I had misunderstood his words.

"Well, I have never given you anything either, so now we're not even," I said.

He laughed.

"Why did you send for me?" I asked, trying to get straight to the point.

"You will not understand this when I tell you, and no matter what you say, you cannot sway my decision."

Ill news. I knew it!

"An initiation is taking place, and it is my time to go. The last one occurred two hundred thirty-nine years ago. It will happen during the ceremony known as Rudiment."

"What do you mean it is your time to go?" I asked, distressed.

"I will explain everything, Thadacus. Please sit down," he said.

I did as he requested, sitting in the wooden chair across from him. "Please, go on."

"Long ago the Ragnvaldr decreed there could be no more than five hundred vampires. We are occasionally compelled to give our magic to another. However, we must seek permission first and wait for the right time. It is time to impart immortality upon a deserving human."

He became quiet, seeming to dive into his own thoughts.

"I know the rule. What I do not understand is why there can only be five hundred immortals. Most importantly, what has this got to do with you?"

"I am one thousand eight hundred fifty-one years old. I have lived, loved, and fulfilled all my desires, both human and vampire. This dream has expired for me. I am ready to accept the next step. Nothing interests me anymore, not even feeding."

"By next step, you mean…?"

"Yes, death. I do not fear it. I invite it; it is something new," said Egan with enthusiasm.

"I have very few friends, Egan. Why do you have to do this? You are being selfish. Why can't they initiate this new vampire and let you be? The rule is stupid."

"You were not here during the great plague. We starved, and some died during that time with our meager five hundred. You have surely studied famines in history. It was known to us as the Bloodless Time.

"Most humans give no thought to how many of them there are. Another plague is due. Through all of their medical advances and technology, they have not learned that lesson. Their leaders do not know how to fix the problem, but nature does. Mark my words. We will be hungry again."

"How many died?" I asked.

"Before it was over, there were three hundred forty-eight of us," responded Egan.

"Wouldn't there have been plenty to eat with all the dead?" I asked, not fully understanding the reasons for the hunger.

"We tried feeding on the tainted blood of the dying, but that did not work. Have you ever smelled the carcass of a rotting animal consumed with gangrene? Well, intensify that three times, and you might understand why we could not feed on these infected humans. The black death spoiled their blood."

"How did the vampires die? Was it starvation?"

"Some of the old ones chose to leave this world so the younger ones could go on. Fights ensued over the right to a meal. Hunger can make our kind do crazy things. Our law of only feeding upon the wicked was broken several occasions. Some of the desperate vampires who had fed upon the blood of innocents could not live with their guilt. They sought penance for their crimes by starving themselves to death. It took longer than a year for their magic to completely leave. They withered away. Their mummified corpses were laid to rest in the Catacombs of Jigh. All vampires are eventually laid to rest there; that is where I shall be buried as well."

I hesitated for a moment but then had to ask. "Did you ever feed upon an innocent human?"

He laughed before responding.

At least he's not offended, I thought.

"No, but I was attacked by another vampire. She and I had been watching the same baron inflict horrible cruelties upon his vassals. He would have them whipped on a regular basis for his own amusement. Can you imagine trying to kill another vampire for the right to feed, but you are both virtually indestructible? It can be done, but it is difficult. Our fight lasted for hours. She was a fierce fighter, as we all are. In the end, I gave her the baron and continued my hunt."

"Who was she?" I asked curiously.

"It is not important. No offense, but I prefer to keep her identity to myself. Like I said, hunger drove her to fight me. I do not blame her."

"How does the Ragnvaldr kill vampires since we are indestructible?"

"Not just any vampire can attend Rudiment. I am not just inviting you. I am giving you special permission to attend. You will learn the secret of a vampire's demise there—and there only. The secret is kept among our ancient ones for a reason, but you, Thadacus, have earned my trust, which is not easily accomplished. I invite you to learn what so many of our kind do not know."

"A vampire had to die so I could be turned?"

"A human was going to be turned regardless. You did not cause the death of a vampire. Dario, the creator of our Ragnvaldr and the one who was compelled to turn me, had become as I now am. He presented his case, and the vampire council took note of his misery and granted his request.

Vampires living across the world were given word a human could be adopted into our clan if there was a desire and consent from the council.

"Illisa was the next to pass on our powers. She loved you and chose to turn you, and I, now, can see why. She had been watching over you for quite some time. One night the compulsion struck her, so you were the lucky one to receive a vampire's magic."

"Then why don't I feel lucky?"

He paused for a moment, and I got the feeling he was not telling me the entire story.

"She sought permission and made her case why you deserved the privilege of becoming one of us, and it was a good one—so good, in fact, I desired to meet you."

"I never see Illissa! She lives as far away from me as possible! I have not seen her even once in the past two hundred thirty-nine years. It is like she was sickened by my presence and had to leave. I remember loving her when I was human, so why does she hate me now?" I asked, becoming upset with her all over again.

"Well, there could be several explanations. First, you are not Illissa's mate. She is with the human, Dane Felder, and has been for a long while. Maybe she loved you in a different way and now she wants to turn Dane but cannot."

I put my head down in shame. *Why had she stopped loving me? Had she ever really loved me? Maybe I was just a game for her…*

Seeing he had embarrassed me, Egan moved on to his second point.

"We occasionally yearn to give our magic to another, as Illissa did with you. We can only turn a few humans. Then both the desire and the ability leave us. We give a piece of ourselves with each bite. Maybe Illissa sees an irretrievable part of her magic in you, so she is saddened by its loss. Maybe it was your destiny to become vampire, so the magic called to her, and she could not control the desire to turn you. To be honest, I envy her. She is still a young vampire and has felt the compulsion, but I, even as old as I am, have never felt the urge to turn a human."

"Why is that so important to you?" I asked.

"There are many reasons, but the most basic explanation is that I have enjoyed being a vampire, and I want to pass the gift along to someone else deserving even though the magic does not call to me. The council has already granted my wish."

"What if it doesn't work since you do not feel compelled?" I asked skeptically.

"Then nothing is lost, but I will still go through the ceremony."

"Who are you going to try to turn?" I pried.

"Come to the ceremony, and you shall see."

"No! I'm furious. I do not condone your decision! What will Savora do once you are gone? How does she feel about this?"

"She has accepted it. She understands we all have our time to go. I have made her miserable as of late because she pleases me no longer. I have no interest in having a mate. She will go on. She is a young vampire with much to still experience."

"I don't have a mate, but I can't understand wanting to leave one behind so easily. What if you are wrong about Savora?" I argued.

Trying to calm myself, I sat back in my chair, closed my eyes, reflecting on the reason for my argument. I did not want to create a relationship with a woman, knowing I could not turn her. I told myself it would not be worth the trouble. It was like adopting a pet and then eventually having to watch it die. I did not want to find love only to give it up, and none of the vampire women I had met appealed to me.

Egan interrupted my thoughts. "I have spoken to Savora, and she accepts my feelings. She tires of me as well, but she will stay with me until I am gone. She looks forward to Rudiment."

Disappointment overwhelmed me.

"Why does it have to be this way? You are committing suicide."

"I believe earth was created for humans and that a special place exists for them after death. I was once human, and I want to enter that place, which for so long has been denied me."

"I don't agree with your decision! I never will! You are throwing your life away!"

"I am always amused by you." He laughed. "You are so young, like a child to me. That is why I enjoy your company. Your energy and passion are invigorating."

"Then spend time with me!" I requested. Maybe I could make him forget about wanting to die.

"I shall. There are still a few days until the ceremony."

I showed my fangs out of frustration.

Egan glared at me for a moment. "Thadacus! I have grown old—not in body but in spirit. It is more gratifying to grant immortality to one who loves life so much—loves it as much as I once did. I will discuss it no further; I grow tired of the subject. It is my turn to ask the questions. How was Europe?"

"Well, since you have lived so long and have seen so much, you should already know the answer to that! Nothing I say could possibly hold any interest for you!"

"Funny, Thadacus! Really funny! Seriously, did you find what you were searching for? Did you discover any ancient relics?"

"A few. They are safely stashed for my later amusement. Sorry I did not bring any of them. I left in a hurry. I was hoping a ghost would visit me, but none did. I now know that they truly do not exist. I searched and stayed in every supposed haunted place but saw nothing. Humans create lies to make money off these ancient sites."

"I have shared this with no one, not even Savora," said Egan, taking a more serious tone. "You are my dear friend, and I want someone to know about this before I go to my grave. Would you like to know something that very few beings are aware of?"

I trained my eyes toward him, not knowing what to expect.

"It is okay to seek the past, to desire it because of its simplicity or codes of honor, but I warn you: do not search for the dead," said Egan, his expression hinting he had seen something unnatural.

"I believe the dead know nothing, especially after living as I have for the past twenty years."

"All manner of magical creatures exist, even spirits," said Egan, pausing to see the look on my face.

"How do you know this?"

"There are spirits that have remained after death, but they are nothing but pure evil."

"Why haven't I seen any of them?"

"You have to open yourself up to them—invite them, welcome them—in order to see them. Nothing good ever comes from their presence. They cannot give anyone anything worth taking."

"Why didn't you tell me this before I left? Was I not in danger?"

"I knew what you were seeking, and there is a difference. These apparitions are often referred to as *demons* by those who have seen them, but they were never human. You only wish to see and experience the human past. No evil can come from that."

"I don't understand. I was seeking the dead!"

"But only the dead of humans! Unfortunately, humans, not vampires, are more likely to see these spirits. They constantly invite them in without understanding the consequences."

"If they were not demons, what were they?" I asked.

"I researched it until I could find no more on the subject. I will admit it occupied my mind for centuries. I believe they are the dead from a magical race once known as the mercurides. There are none now living, at least not in this realm. They require humans to do their bidding."

"How do you know?"

"It is speculation after much research. I believe the evil ones are only a small percentage of the entire race. From my studies, I have concluded they were banished or trapped in this realm, and they especially have a vengeance for humans."

"Why humans?"

"I think humans caused their current state."

"So how is it you know of the mercurides, but the rest of us are still in the dark?"

Egan frowned. "No one ever really asked how it was that I became vampire. Everyone knows Dario was compelled to turn me, but the old ones who knew my story are all gone now. It is a sore memory for me."

Egan stopped speaking for a moment and gathered his composure. I could tell this was hard for him. I started to say, "You don't have to tell me," but I couldn't get the words out. I was too engrossed in his story and fascinated by the existence of other realms and magical creatures.

"I have personally seen a mercuride, and I have known no greater terror. Let us just say when I was human, I dabbled in things I should not have. It is how I discovered others with great intelligence, besides humans, inhabit earth. A mercuride picked up on my favorite pastime, pursuing the unknown. I had discovered its existence; so naturally, I wanted to know more about it. I encouraged its company. I got what I had wished for. The mercuride known as Salumus began to relentlessly follow me. He wanted me to do his dirty work.

"People thought I was deranged, had lost my mind. When Dario discovered me, I was contemplating suicide. I wanted rid of Salumus. There was no end to his tortures. Dario could not see this vile spirit, but after befriending me and after countless conversations trying to talk me out of killing myself, he too began to feel Salumus's presence.

"He needed no permission to turn me. There were very few vampires during his time. He did not know what would happen after the turning, but I think he was hoping it would give him sight of the creature."

"Was Dario able to see Salumus afterward?"

"No. Once I became vampire, the mercuride deserted me. I was not human anymore, so I became of no interest to the monster."

"Why are they not interested in a vampire's help?" I asked. Egan hesitated.

"I will share this with you because I am leaving. Although it may not seem like a huge secret, I would ask you keep it anyway. Consider it my last wish and gift to you. Promise me after my response you will ask no more questions."

"I swear!" I said without hesitation.

"I believe our magic comes from the same realm. Dario continued to research the mercurides, but I wanted no part of it. I inherited Dario's diaries, most of which contained his thoughts regarding the vile wraiths, but I avoided reading them for several hundred years—until I finally accepted my abilities and strengths as a vampire and feared Salumus no longer. However, I think I would shudder at the sight of one even to this day. I can say no more," said Egan, shivering slightly.

"Then let us speak of it no more."

"Wise decision! I almost regret telling you about them. It's like I have exposed my child to an unnecessary evil, now that I see the look upon your face," he said regretfully.

I took a deep breath. "No, do not think that. It was an interesting story. Thank you."

"I am hungry. How do you feel about hunting?" Egan asked, standing up from his favorite chair.

I nodded.

"Savora may want to join us. Do you mind?"

I did not respond quickly. My mind was racing with the things Egan had just told me, but also my thoughts were on Rhymee. A fear gripped me. Suddenly I felt like something would happen to the child, and I would not be there to protect her. She was gifted with insight, seeing deeper meaning in the world surrounding her, but why was I obsessing over the child? I found it odd that I was attached to her.

"I am sorry. What?"

"There is something else, isn't there? I see it written on your face. What is on your mind, Thadacus?"

"Nothing important really..."

"There has to be. Otherwise you would not be dwelling on it," he pointed out.

"Oh, it's really nothing. During my journey through rural Arkansas, I stopped in a field. A small, two-storey house lay in the distance. The family that lived there stepped out to enjoy the night. I was famished, but I quickly discerned they were good people. They had a little girl that shocked me. She knew I was watching her, but she couldn't see me, or so I thought. I would swear she had magical powers of some kind, like X-ray vision or clairvoyance."

"How do you know she could see you?" asked Egan, interested.

"She instructed me to look at the moon. I was hiding, and she looked right in my direction," I explained, still astounded.

"Could she have been talking to another animal in the vicinity or to herself?"

I replayed the scene over again in my mind and remembered the look she had given me. "No, I am convinced she was speaking to me. At first, I tried to think of an explanation for the occurrence, but now I find my thoughts drifting to her. I know she is different, and I am drawn to her because of it."

Egan curled his index finger then chewed on it as he thought for a moment. "I suggest you keep your eye on this one. Protect her. I think it is no coincidence you crossed paths. I don't know why I feel this way, but that is my advice," he said, giving me a deep look.

I took pleasure in hunting with Egan and Savora. We sniffed out a serial killer, one who was really sick in the head. We came upon his work first, a backyard full of decayed flesh and bones.

"This is another sign a plague is coming," said Egan, inspecting a femur. "Serial killers are quite common. They are the result of a warning from nature. A prequel to what is coming."

We waited days for the white male in his late fifties to make his move on an unsuspecting child. We wanted to make sure we had tracked the right one.

I was so angry with his actions I delighted in torturing him. We took turns feeding, but Egan fed first. He seemed distant and disinterested. After Savora had her fill, I threw salt over my shoulder then was the last one to drain the killer's blood.

"What is wrong?" I asked.

"I must return. The ceremony is tomorrow."

I followed Egan home, grabbed my diary, and told my friend good-bye.

"Stay. The ceremony is something you need to see," he suggested.

"I cannot bear to see you in pain, and I do not have any desire to watch your death."

"But, Thadacus, that is why you need to be there. You understand so very little. We feel no pain when we die as vampires. Pain was only felt during our human life."

"I do not want to add that memory to my list. I will miss you so…"

"I understand. I hold no hard feelings. Even after I am gone, you will always be welcome here."

I left quickly.

For a moment, I stood at the end of the lane. Did I desire to return to Europe? As I slowly began to walk, I knew the answer was no. I was inclined to follow the same path back to the little, white farmhouse. I realized Egan was right, and I suddenly wanted to seize his advice. I did not want to smother this desire as I had so many others. I gave into it. I allowed the yearning to see Rhymee consume me.

LEAVING

1981

For nine years, I watched over Rhymee and her family. I could hear the slightest noises at great distances, and I could tell what they were up to just by listening. I came to know the Stewarts through the decisions they made in everyday life. Richard was good to his children, yet he did not spare the rod when they needed to learn life's harsh lessons. He made sure his family spent time together; they were close. I was impressed by their devotion. I had been orphaned by age sixteen and had to fend for myself. My mother died giving birth to my sister, and she in turn died before she was a year old, of small pox. My father made me what I am now, but he had very little time to do it. He worked from sun up to sun down to support the two of us until he began to lose weight and cough uncontrollably. He was already worn thin when the tuberculosis struck. He died quickly of the disease.

Although I was cared for, I never experienced the closeness the Stewarts had. My family had not been given the opportunity. Richard and Bhren were kind and generous. Richard once gave an intoxicated, cold vagabond his coat and Bible, hoping it would help the guy. Hours afterward, the drunk, reeking of whiskey, fell asleep on some train tracks and was killed.

The gift ended up getting Richard in trouble with the law because his name was stitched on the tag inside the coat, and his address and phone numbers were written on the front page of his Bible. Detectives questioned him for weeks before they finally decided Richard had nothing to do with the man's untimely death. I believe even after going through all of that, he would still not hesitate helping someone in need. His family never questioned his innocence. They stood by him until the matter was resolved.

Rhymee's mother, Bhren, was a truly innocent person. Because her views of the world remained constant, I often knew how she would respond when it concerned matters of importance regarding her family and friends. She had a strong sense of right and wrong, yet she was not vengeful and accepted life good or bad as the way of things.

Rhymee had two younger sisters. Rhondel was the middle child, and Rhegan was the youngest.

Each child had special talents, leading them each in different directions.

Rhondel was a stout child with brownish-gold eyes and hair. At five years old, she was loyal to her friends and family, but if someone hurt her, she never forgot. She always took up for her older sister, sometimes getting herself in trouble.

Rhegan had steel-gray eyes with blonde hair and numerous freckles. She carried a natural light. She had the ability to cheer others up when they were at their lowest. Even at age two, she could cool her father's temper and get away with things her two older sisters could not.

I had grown to love the Stewarts, but I held a special place in my heart for Rhymee. She looked at the world in a different way and detected things the others could not. A falling star, to most, was just a natural occurrence, but to her it was magical and held deeper meaning.

By day, I would meditate in the shaft of an old well near the farmhouse. I often thought about my victims. Had I hunted them for the right reasons? It was not the most comfortable topic to think about, but the deep hole was secluded, which suited my mood. I enjoyed the smell of the moss and earth covering the damp rocks lining the walls. The well had been dry for ages, but sometimes during rainy springs, the bottom would pool up, amplifying the sounds from above ground.

I rarely came out during the day because vampires are naturally nocturnal, blinded by sunlight. Our eyes can detect the slightest motion through the darkness. My favorite time to hunt was when there was no moon and stars, during a cloud-covered, wintry night.

I stayed near Rhymee as much as possible. I became agitated when she would leave for school or when I had to hunt. Sometimes my prey would lead me on a two- to three-day journey.

For some reason, Rhymee's senses caused her to become more and more introverted with each passing year. She had seen death's work when she was eight, with the passing of her grandfather. It made her aware of her own mortality and fragility.

One evening, when she had just turned eleven, I leapt from the well to guard her. I listened closely. She had been told to take out the garbage and dump it in the field. I heard her heart hammering, and she was breathing to the point of hyperventilation. She was scared of something. Did she fear the darkness?

"But, Mom, can't I do it in the morning before school?" she begged.

"No! I need to wash that plate!" said Bhren, losing her patience.

"But—" said Rhymee, trying to think of an excuse. "I'll wash it in the morning. I promise!"

"Do it now! Quit being lazy, Rhymee!" said Bhren.

Rhymee's heart began to race faster.

"Rhymee! Do as your mother says!" barked Richard.

Rhymee jumped at her father's orders. She loved her dad with all her heart, but she also respected him.

She grabbed the plate of garbage and headed for the living room. Rhondel was sitting on the couch, engrossed in a movie on television.

"Please come with me to take out the garbage," Rhymee politely requested.

"I did it last night," whined Rhondel. "Besides, I don't want to miss this part."

"Sweetie, there is nothing out there going to get you. Would it help if I turned on the porch light?" asked Richard.

I stood behind the barn and watched. Rhymee took a deep breath, and I could smell her nervous sweat before she opened the front door. She tiptoed quietly, trying to reach her destination undetected. She stopped halfway in the front yard, tempted to dump the garbage there. I heard her shaking and the plate slipping from her grip. She almost dropped it.

"Mom and Dad will be disappointed in me. I can do this," she said to herself.

Reaching the edge of the field, she quietly raked the leftover spaghetti to the ground. She paused to look at the starlit sky and briefly gathered her composure then looked in my direction. I quickly moved out of sight, behind a tree.

I heard her stomach beginning to churn. Then she swallowed deeply to either suppress her fear or nausea. She knew I was there, and she feared me.

Her dog came running up behind her. She quickly turned, expecting the worst. When she realized it was only Old Blue, she wanted to pass out, but she somehow found the strength to run back in the house.

Inevitably, almost every night she would enter into a trance-like state where her dreams controlled her mind and body, causing her to either wet the bed or walk in her sleep. One morning, she woke in her mother's car, not knowing how she had gotten there. That gave her parents a scare, and on another occasion, she had a rude awakening in the bath tub. However, most nights she woke to find herself outside in the front yard.

It was a hard decision, but I decided to leave. Egan had been wrong about this, just like he had been wrong to die. I was only causing her misery; I was causing her to be terrified of the dark. The night before I departed, I made sure the well was covered so Rhymee and her sisters could not fall in. I inspected the yard and surrounding area for dangers and made things as safe as I could. I entered her parents' room and spoke to them in their sleep, warning them to keep her in a locked room at night so she couldn't exit the house without their help. I knew my spell would work and they would listen.

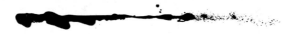

For four years, I again traveled through Europe and checked on my artifacts. One token was a miniature likeness of Thor's hammer, Mjollnir, cast in iron. It was originally part of a necklace worn by a Samis pagan to show his devotion to the Norse god of thunder. He had met his doom, along with several of his comrades, when the Christians invaded the Scandinavian town of Lovon. His beheaded skull and body were on the verge of being excavated from one of the many burial mounds dotting the countryside. I had been fortunate enough to dig it up before the humans were able to.

This small token had been meant as a gift for Egan. While holding the small piece of iron and admiring its intricate detail, my thoughts drifted to my old friend as they often did. I remembered his home in Hammond and suddenly had a desire to return there. He did, after all, say I would be welcome anytime. I didn't know how Savora would feel about my unexpected arrival, but I didn't care. I would give the hammer to her since she had inherited most everything else of Egan's. I found many artifacts strewn across the lands from ancient history. The plunder was supposed to act as a distraction so I would not dwell on Rhymee. I was trying to forget her, but I couldn't. I hid the hoard in my cavern, which I had discovered along the coast of the North Sea. Only a deep-sea diver or another vampire would have had the ability to discover it; its mouth was beneath the surface of the ocean. I sometimes compared myself to the old, hard-scaled, treasure-hoarding dragons from many stories and myths, laughing at my odd similarities. I was just as comfortable and right at home as any cranky, lonely dragon would be.

I again suffered an airplane ride so I could return to America. This time I took a shorter route and landed at Little Rock National Airport.

A black cat crossed my path, so I went through the motions of spitting in my hair, right as Savora greeted me in the courtyard. She must have been standing outside for hours in the deep snow listening to it fall from the sky.

"Thad, you are funny. I saw you performing one of your old-fashioned superstitions. Wiping spit in your hair is disgusting." Savora laughed.

"Humm."

"What brings you my way?" she asked welcomingly.

"I was thinking of Egan, so I wanted to visit. How have you been, Savora?" I asked. I was only revealing half the truth. I simply wanted to be in the same country as Rhymee. Through the years abroad, my longing to see her had been torturous. I often wondered how she had grown. What did she look like now? Had she overcome her fears? Had her insight blossomed even more? I told myself over and over again that it was best to stay away, but dreams of her consumed my days. I had to check on her.

"It rarely snows here. Ssshhh! Listen! It sounds like someone's tapping a tiny xylophone as the flakes knock into each other and hit the branches of the trees and the ground."

I did as I was instructed, and for another hour, I stood motionless and enjoyed the sound of snowflakes falling. Before we shook it off, we had disappeared, becoming a camouflaged part of the snow-covered landscape.

I suddenly caught the smell of an unfamiliar vampire. I became tense and looked around. He must have visited before the snowstorm.

Savora shook her chestnut hair and blinked a few times to clear her violet eyes of ice then answered my question.

"Nothing interesting has happened for quite some time."

"Who has visited? I do not recognize the scent."

"Michael Horn. I befriended him while on a trip to New York, after Egan's departure. He is quite a talented painter. I have several of his pieces inside. His memories come to life on canvass. Would you like to meet him?" she asked.

"He is here?"

"He is inside."

I decided before ever meeting this Michael that I disliked him. I immediately felt he must be taking advantage of Savora and Egan's estate and wealth.

I looked away from her into the foreboding forest. "I cannot stay," I said, clinching my hands into fists. *Stinking mooch*, I thought.

"You are not making any sense. You obviously had time to waste here in the yard, so you can come in."

I couldn't give her a quick answer unless I told her the truth, so I looked down to avoid eye contact.

"Why can't you look at me, Thad?" she asked.

Instead of looking up at her, I sourly glanced at the house.

Savora had a quick wit, and within seconds she knew I had a problem with her newfound friend.

"You think he is taking advantage of me, don't you?"

Finally my eyes met hers. "How do you know he isn't? Egan would not like it."

"Egan is gone. What he would have wanted no longer matters. He left the estate to me, and I am no fool, Thad."

She had a point, but I still didn't want to give in to her.

"Thad, Egan is not coming back. What do you expect? I can't live in solitude like you do. Do you not get lonely?"

I began to slouch. Suddenly I was depressed. She was asking me questions I did not want to answer. I closed my eyes to contain my emotions and regain my composure. I didn't want to admit I was wrong.

"Please, Thad, come in and meet him."

"I don't see what the big deal is. What so great about him? So he is an artist. I have met plenty of those that probably did better work," I responded bitterly.

"Thad, he's my mate!"

Suddenly my hatred included her. How could she forget Egan so easily? Why had I come here?

Dang it! I'm too late! I can't escape him now! I thought as a platinum blonde, overly tanned, barely-out-of-his-teens vampire bailed out the front door and rudely interrupted Savora and me.

"I am assuming you are Thadacus Goodridge. I have heard a lot about you. Nice to finally meet you," stated Michael, holding out his hand.

I declined the offer. "I can't stay!" I said to Savora.

"What's the rush? You're a vampire; you have all the time in the world," said Michael.

"How would you know of my affairs or know my schedule?" Michael shrugged.

"At least come inside and let me show you some of my work."

"I am sure I have seen similar paintings."

"I'm sure you haven't! I take my work very seriously," said Michael.

What the…? I can't believe the nerve of this guy! I thought.

"Enough! Thadacus, I am ashamed of you! How could you be so rude?" asked Savora.

"It's okay, Savora. I understand his behavior," Michael interjected.

"You do? Then enlighten me since you know so much," I responded.

"I would be happy to. You hate me because you're in love with Savora and I have stolen your chance with her. Is that hitting the head of the nail?" he asked, sneering.

I laughed in spite of myself. I really was acting childish.

Savora did not think it was funny. "Egan would be ashamed of you, Thad!"

She was right.

"Oh come on. I am just kidding, dude," said Michael, jabbing at my arm.

"Dude"? What kind of language was that? I thought.

Savora had definitely mated with her polar opposite.

"Where are you from, Michael?" I asked.

"California, but I fell in love with New York so later moved there. Why? What about you?"

I didn't answer him. I didn't owe him anything; I was his elder. Even though I was a younger vampire, I was older in human years. He looked as if he were barely twenty.

"Well, I am ready to go inside. I am finished talking in the snow," said Savora.

"And I am not coming in."

"If you can't come in, then don't come back!" said Savora sharply.

I had hurt her feelings, and I felt like a jackass. I ended up going inside partly because I felt guilty and partly because I wanted to check on Egan's things. I had to make sure Savora had taken care of his library and, most of all, his chair.

Over the next few days, I warmed up to Michael. Egan's death wasn't this young vampire's fault. His soul was pure, and I soon found out he had his own fortune and nice apartment. He and Savora traveled between Hammond and New York City often. I had gotten lucky by catching them here. I realized I was really angry with Egan for leaving me, but that was pointless. He was dead. The house constantly reminded me of him. His stamps and ancient coins were framed and hung on every wall. His journals and books were still stacked disorderly along shelves and desks throughout the house, and they reeked of his scent. Savora had not touched them. I could not enter a room without being reminded of his love of collecting. After a week, I had to leave.

"Where are you headed?" asked Savora, stopping me at the door. "In case I need to reach you."

"Prairie Grove, Arkansas, but I will only be there for a night before I return to England. You know where to send my mail."

"Take care, Thadacus."

I turned to walk out. "I am sorry I was so rude. It won't happen on our next encounter."

"You are forgiven," she said.

"Wait!" shouted Michael from the staircase. "I wish to give you something!" He came down and handed me a miniature sketch pad and a package containing two charcoal pencils.

"It is lightweight, easy to carry!"

"I am no artist," I said, flipping the blank pages of the pad.

"You might surprise yourself," he said.

I nodded in appreciation. "I do have a request, if you don't mind?"

"Shoot," said Michael, excited he could be of service to me in any way.

"Take care of Savora. Don't ever abandon her, all right?"

"You don't even have to ask. I wouldn't dream of it."

"I can take care of myself. I have been quite successful at it for a lot longer than you," she said with an air of superiority.

"I still worry about you."

"Well, you shouldn't," she said, but I could see through her tough demeanor. She appreciated my concern.

When I got down the lane, I stopped and pulled the miniature Mjollnir from my pocket. I could not give it to Savora. It would just become a dusty piece of her inheritance. I knew someone else who might grow to appreciate it more.

NIGHTS AND DAYS

"Rhymee, what is it?" my parents would always ask.

"I don't know. I just…" I was plagued with bad dreams on a nightly basis, but the covers were my security. Every night I pulled them over my head and pushed them upward into a dome shape so I could breathe easier. I imagined I was in a rock fortress where nothing could harm me. Summer nights at my parents' farmhouse were miserable. I grew so hot I was drenched in sweat, but I would not give up my covers for any reason, not even when they became damp and clammy.

I didn't like getting out of bed during the night for any reason, not even to get a drink. Shadows from chairs, toys, tree limbs, and window shutters came to life at night, dancing back and forth along the walls of my bedroom. Occasionally, the silhouettes terrified me so much that I broke out in hives.

Sometimes I walked in my sleep. I'd wake up in strange places, like the bathtub, my parents' car, out on the front porch, but I had no memory of how I'd gotten there. On the nights I didn't sleepwalk, I wet the bed because I couldn't wake from these deep trances. I often sat up in bed screaming with my eyes closed while I was still asleep, but sometimes I was awake and deliberately cried out so my parents would come and rescue me.

They would try to reassure me.

"Can I sleep with you?" I felt bad because I knew I would crowd them, but their answer was always yes until my sisters were born and became old enough to sleep with me.

The slightest noises, such as the house settling, acorns hitting the roof, or pings against the windowpane would send me into trembling states of hysteria. I did not believe my parents when they told me nothing was out there lurking in the darkness. My instincts begged me to fear something, but what, I didn't know. There was an ill presence mainly in the darkness, but sometimes I could feel it in the light of day. A breeze sometimes would pick up and blow during a hot, still day, only in secluded spots, causing me to shiver. I looked around trying to discover its source, but I'd find nothing.

Rhondel often noticed my distractions. She'd ask me what was wrong.

"Do you see or feel anything in the sky or in the forest?" I always asked her.

She searched intently and would tell me I was scaring her. I didn't want to talk about my foolish notions, so I'd lie to her and tell her I was playing a game and that she was no fun. She said I was weird quite often.

There were times when I felt safe. It was on those days I mustered enough courage to practice riding my bike along the dirt road leading to town or on the lane stretching between my Aunt Hada's house and ours. I trusted it to carry me quickly. It moved faster than I could run, so it was one of my favorite possessions. It was on one of these bike rides that I became aware of an enticing, sweet yet harsh odor lingering around the farm. Was it a strange plant growing in the area? I came close a few times to locating its source, but I never could. I asked my parents and sisters if they could smell it. The answer was always no, and they would look at me strangely, like I was off my rocker.

At first, I assumed the scent was a natural part of the landscape, but I later realized it wasn't caused by the odor of a plant blooming in the spring. The odor remained throughout winter, but it wasn't present all the time. It came and went, and when it left, it was gone for three to four days at a time, and then it would return.

I came to love this euphoric odor. I hated when it left. I didn't feel as terrified when I smelled that scent. Somehow it seemed to keep my fear at bay.

One gloomy morning I stepped outside and took a deep breath. Whatever had caused the odor was gone. I assumed it would return within a few days as it usually did, so I patiently waited, tolerating the feeling that invisible monsters were lurking in the frightening air surrounding our farm. I was heartbroken when I realized it wasn't coming back. Had I done something to cause its absence?

"Please come back," I quietly begged when no one else was listening. "I need you."

There was no response to my pleas, so I again became reclusive, seeking security from the confines of the house and my blankets.

The nightmares became worse, yet I couldn't remember much about them when I woke. My mother grew tired of washing my bedding every day, so she took me to see my pediatrician. I was put on a strict regimen of no water after supper, and I had to eat lots of crackers before bedtime. My parents talked about taking me to a counselor, but I begged them not to. I did not like hospital and doctor visits, so they didn't make me go. I told them that I didn't feel crazy. I felt normal, but isn't that how crazy people thought?

THE ACCIDENT

1985

Even though I made good time after leaving Egan's house, the trip seemed like a long one. The closer I came to Prairie Grove, the more eager I became. After crossing the state line, I could not go fast enough. It was gloomy, and clouds darkened the sky. I could see comfortably through my sunglasses, so I kept traveling, even after daylight.

I reached the farm as the school bus pulled up to the edge of the Stewarts' driveway. I watched from the edge of the woods. My black shirt and blue jeans blended well against the murky light of the shrouded forest. I stood straight and merged with the many tree trunks surrounding me. Rhegan, Rhondel, and Rhymee quickly bounded down the steps and then stopped to take deep breaths like they'd just been released from prison. I was surprised by how much the girls had grown. Rhymee's hair brushed the small of her back. Her almond eyes carried a sultry, serious look. Her perfectly contoured, thin lips matched her sylphlike body. She stopped and took a deep breath, staring in my direction. I was so ferociously drawn to her I had to grasp the tree for support. I fought against revealing myself. I wanted to show her I was real and that I would not hurt her.

"Rhymee, come on! Let's play in the snow!" shouted Rhondel.

Rhymee gazed at the forest for a moment longer then turned her attention to her sisters. "Coming!"

The snow was deep, so the girls took their time going into the house. They began to make snowballs and throw them at each other.

Rhegan was the first to get hit, so she ran inside after only a few minutes. Rhymee and Rhondel stayed outside until the aroma of dinner began to overpower the clear, wintry air.

The sisters did everything they could think of with the freshly fallen snow. They made sure every section of untouched, smooth ground was covered with tracks. I laughed quietly to myself until they came a little too close to the dense cedar tree I was hiding behind.

Rhymee stopped her sister from taking another step. "We should stay near the house." Her voice had changed from a child's high pitch to serious and unwavering. I craved to hear it again.

Rhondel didn't question her older sister. Once they reached the front yard, they again began to play.

When they could not stand the sting of snowballs any longer, they stopped and made snow angels, then a snowman, and then attempted an igloo.

"Come on, Rhondel. Help me gather the snow for another block," ordered Rhymee, knowing her time to play was running out.

"Hold on!" yelled Rhondel, taking off her glove.

Rhondel's fingers were purple from the cold.

"What are you doing? We aren't going to finish this tonight unless you help me!" exclaimed Rhymee, breathing heavy puffs of vapor.

"I'm going inside. I don't care if we finish it tonight. My fingers, face, and toes hurt," griped Rhondel, briskly rubbing her checks. "Anyway, I'm sure Mom has supper ready. I can smell hamburgers. It's time to come in."

I could see Rhymee rub her gloves together and blow her hot breath at the tips of her fingers, and then she would wince. I felt sorry for her. I remembered suffering from the cold when I was human and found it odd that I no longer was affected by the elements.

"I'll come inside in a moment," said Rhymee, suppressing the pain in her fingers. She was going to finish her igloo. I was amazed by her perseverance. She was not a quitter.

I could hear her sigh deeply when Bhren opened the door. I don't think she was aware of how cold Rhymee really was.

"Rhymee, run down to your aunt's house and get some salt. We've run out."

Rhymee's aunt, Hada Dowell, lived on a dirt lane about a quarter mile away. There were cow pastures on each side of the lane. One belonged to the Stewarts and the other to the Dowells.

"Rhymee, hurry back! We are waiting to eat, and it's almost dark!"

Rhymee jumped on her bike at her mother's orders. "Yes, ma'am!"

The temperature was dropping. Her hands and feet must have been numb.

Checking on her had not satisfied my worries and curiosity; it made them worse. I was single minded in preserving her well-being. I ran alongside her from behind the tree line of the forest located beyond the Stewarts' field. I was troubled. I could smell a winter storm approaching.

Without grass acting as an insulator and gravel absorbing the sun's heat, the lane was surprisingly clear with a few ice patches here and there. There were numerous potholes, which had filled with water before the rain had turned to snow and were frozen solid.

"Hmm, ice-skating ponds," she said aloud to herself.

I have never met someone so tenacious, I thought.

She got off her bike and tried to twirl like a professional skater on top of one for a moment. Her stomach began to gurgle loudly, so she hopped back on her bike and continued her journey.

She knocked on her aunt's door. She was shivering uncontrollably.

Hada came to the front door with a warm smile and a box of salt.

"Your mom called. I knew you were on the way. Come inside a moment and warm up."

"Thank you," said Rhymee, eyeing the sky.

It was only a few minutes before the last of the sun's light would fade over the horizon and be replaced by darkness and abysmal weather.

"I love you, Aunt Hada, but I'd better go. They're waiting on me to eat."

I could tell she was more worried about the approaching night.

"Well, come again soon. Lena wants to show you her new record. By the way, call me when you get back. Otherwise I will be worried. You look miserable, child."

"I'm okay," replied Rhymee, grabbing the box of salt and shoving it in her coat pocket. It stuck out awkwardly, but it would have to do.

Pedaling hard and fast, she raced back up the lane, dodging ice patches along the way.

Her shoelaces were untied, but she ignored them. They were wet and chunked over with ice. Besides, her fingers must have been too cold to tie her shoes. I wished I could carry her in my arms.

She hit a bump, and the box of salt was almost knocked from her pocket. She was concentrating on securing the salt and failed to realize her left shoestring had been wrapping around the end of her pedal. Suddenly the pedal wouldn't turn.

She looked down for only a moment to see what had caused her constriction, and she lost her balance. Her handlebars began to pull, at first only slightly side to side, but the jerks grew wider with each attempt to recover control. Her bike had suddenly turned against her, like a bucking horse.

Abruptly, she veered to the left and crashed hard into the barbed-wire fence. The barbs cut through the soft skin of her upper chest, legs, and arms. She lay across her bike awkwardly. Her ankle was obviously broken.

She wailed from the pain, but no one heard her, except for me.

"Momma! Daddy!" she cried, hoping her family would come to her rescue.

I raced from the woods to behind the barn. I feared I would terrify her. I had to find a way to help her without revealing myself.

Soon Rhymee stopped screaming and made no sound. I panicked. Was she unconscious?

Rhegan stepped out on the front porch, searching for signs of her sister.

"Come on, Rhymee. I'm starving," said Rhegan in a hushed voice, pacing back and forth.

"Rhymee is badly injured up the road. Run and tell your parents," I whispered into the night's chilling breeze over and over, hoping she would get the message without waiting to discover its source.

Rhegan stopped pacing and stood there for a few minutes, seeming to think about something, then quickly ran inside.

Thank goodness! My message has reached her, I thought.

"Rhymee is badly injured up the road!" repeated Rhegan, just as I had instructed.

"How do you know?" asked Bhren skeptically.

Rhegan paused. "I don't know," she said, seeming confused.

"Come to think of it, she has been gone a while," said Bhren, sounding worried and looking out the window.

"Call Hada and see if she is there," suggested Richard.

I stood outside the kitchen window, intently listening. When Hada confirmed Rhymee had left and should have reached home, the entire family raced to find her.

They piled into Old Green, Richard's weathered farm truck from the early fifties. It didn't start when someone wanted it to. This was one of those times.

"Oh, I will just run up there!" said Bhren, angrily flinging the door open. "There's no time for this! I shouldn't have sent her alone!"

"Got it!" exclaimed Richard when the engine finally turned over.

Rhymee looked lifeless when they came upon her, but when the headlights of the truck glared in her face, she slowly lifted her head.

"Mom, Dad, I'm sorry. I ruined the salt," Rhymee apologized, fearing she was in trouble.

"Of all things to be worried about," said Richard, carefully cutting her shoestring from the pedal.

As soon as she was free, Richard lifted her up and threw his coat around her.

"Can you stand on it?" he asked, gently lowering her to the ground.

Rhymee silently cried tears of pain and shook her head.

"We'll have to get her to the emergency room." Bhren sighed. "Rhegan, you and Rhondel will have to stay with your aunt until we get back.

"But we want to go too," whined Rhondel. "I don't want to stay with Aunt Hada."

"You're going to Hada's. There's no room in the truck!" replied Bhren sternly.

I had decided to stay until Rhymee's injury had completely healed, but the well no longer seemed inviting. I took a chance and meditated in the barn. I needed meditation, a vampire's form of sleep, even if my thoughts were not always pleasant. I could hear the slightest noise and move quickly if I needed to. I only worried about covering my tracks.

Over the next week, I realized Rhymee not only sensed my presence, but she also sensed something else outside. She was confined to the house to give her cuts time to heal. Most of the day, she would lie in bed and stare out the window toward the barn.

A few days after her accident, I was deep in thought when I heard her grab her crutches and hobble toward the front door. She stopped at the edge of the porch, resting on her good foot.

I patiently listened.

She stood there silently until she began to shiver.

"I don't know if you can hear me, but I know you're out there. What are you? I know you left for a while, and now you're back. I've thought about you all day, and I know you have been here since I was a child. I can usually sense whether a creature is good or bad. I feel you mean me no harm. It's not you I fear—it's something else. When you're here, it seems to stay away for longer periods of time, so whatever your reasons were before, please don't leave us again," she requested. She stood there for a long time, waiting for an answer, and then she hobbled back into her room.

I was in shock. Was she speaking to me? How did she know I was there? How did she know I had been watching over her? I yearned to talk to her but finally refrained from it. Something inside me told me to wait. It wasn't the right time, but I would do as she had requested and never again leave her, except to hunt.

That night, quite late, I watched the stars from the roof of the house. The girls were fast asleep until Rhymee woke with a wet bed, yet again. It was the fourth time within two weeks she had soaked her linens from a nightmare.

"Rhondel, can I sleep with you?" she quietly whispered, trying not to wake her parents.

"Oh, not again," complained Rhondel, not wanting to scoot over. "Go sleep with Rhegan."

Rhymee hesitated to wake Rhegan. There was a chance her youngest sister would go tell her parents, and then she would be in trouble.

I could hear her limp to the window and take several deep breaths out of frustration, and then slowly her breathing sounded restless as she began pacing. I knew she was insecure.

After a while, I could hear her yawn, and she grew sleepy and decided to pull some covers from her bed and sleep the rest of the night on the floor by the heater vent. She turned and was going to hobble back to her bed to retrieve a blanket when she heard a sharp sound against the windowpane that sounded like a rock hitting the glass.

I heard the sound and immediately searched the ground from the roof. I saw or heard nothing else so dismissed the sound as harmless.

Rhymee instantaneously broke out into a sweat and crept to her sister.

"Rhondel, wake up!" she pleaded, shaking her sister.

"Now what?" asked Rhondel, crankier than before.

"Something bad is outside. I heard it," explained Rhymee in an extremely low voice. "What do we do?"

"There's nothing outside. It's your imagination."

"Go look for me."

"Fine. I'm not scared. You're a chicken! Promise me you'll go back to sleep if I do," insisted Rhondel.

"But what if you see something?" asked Rhymee, still terrified.

"You hear things outside all the time, and nothing's ever there!" exclaimed Rhondel, darting to the window and flinging the curtains back.

"Don't do that. It can see you!"

Rhondel stood there looking out the window, searching for signs of a window peeper.

"See, I told you. Nothing's out there. Now go to sleep, and don't wake me up again, or I'll tell Mom and Dad!"

I watched her through a small skylight. She grabbed the top blanket, which was still dry, from the bed and threw it on the floor next to her sister. Even through the thickness of the walls, I could smell her break into a sweat. She must have grown too hot, but not for any reason would she come out from under the blanket. It was her security and provided a place to hide.

I leaped from the roof and searched the area but saw no indication of human or animal having been anywhere in the yard, but the air did feel strangely different. I grew uneasy and kept watch the rest of the night underneath the window.

For three nights in a row, Rhymee's bed-wetting continued, and on the third night, she broke out in hives. She became withdrawn from everyone. She feared the night and was not getting much sleep. Rhondel was, in a way, right. Rhymee had been suffering for years with a fear of the dark and a fear of something else—something not even she understood or could explain.

I thought long and hard. I had the power to help her, but there was a price. Most humans, after being bitten, would develop cancerlike symptoms in their late sixties or early seventies. At that age, their bodies were not strong enough to continue to hold the magic. It would eventually work against them. I had to choose a path, and so I did. Rhymee lived in terror every night and sometimes even during the day. She trusted very few people and was antisocial at school, never participating in extracurricular activities. She had a few close friends that she had known since first grade, but she had trouble making new ones. She even, on rare occasions, distrusted her mom, dad, and sisters. When she felt this way, she would go off cry and pray, attempting to clear her mind of the bad thoughts. I made my decision; I was compelled to bite her. I did not need approval from the council to bite her for the first time. The initial bite would not turn her into a vampire.

A vampire's first bite gave humans the power to see clearly and fearlessly and the power to heal. Human folklore had given my kind a bad reputation over the years. Not many humans have had the pleasure of knowing a vampire and living to tell the tale, but one misconception was our bites were venomous. Quite the contrary, our fangs held magic not poison—a magic that had been passed down from vampire to vampire through the ages.

I did not know where the first vampire originated from. Only the council elder held the knowledge, and only the council leaders could pass the knowledge down to their successors. Egan had been a council leader, and it was tempting on my visits with him to ask, but deep down I knew better.

I knew this magic could cure Rhymee, giving her the strength to face her fears, yet she would still know when she was in real danger.

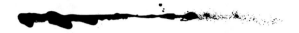

I crept into the small attic window then slid down the wooden retractable ladder, which allowed access to the lower level rooms. As usual, Rhymee was tossing and turning. I quickly leaned over her and breathed. My breath acted like an anesthesia for humans, and she fell into a deep sleep. I then crept over to Rhegan and Rhondel and breathed on them too, just to be safe.

"Rhymee, I am going to bite your leg and help your wound. You will feel a slight sting, but do not wake until morning for any reason," I murmured into her ear. All vampires held the power of hypnosis.

I wasted no time. I bit into her injured leg so no one would notice the fang marks. I willed my magic to transfer to her. I had to swallow a small amount of her blood to seal the pact. It tasted bitter. This shocked me, so I hesitated for a moment. It was not what I had expected from such a sweet child.

Rhymee flinched from the sting of the bite but followed my instruction and did not wake. When I was finished, I left the house and kept watch again underneath her window. Had I done the right thing? I asked myself that question over and over again throughout the night, but I felt that I had.

FEELING UNUSUAL

After I bit Rhymee, I had a mental connection to her. I could not read every thought in her mind, but I could detect her emotional state. I could tell what she was feeling. While she was asleep, I could see her dreams. While awake, if she day-dreamed, it was like I was there, visiting past memories or fantasies with her.

Rhymee felt peculiar and impatient when she woke. It was sunny but still cold. Usually, she dreaded pulling the covers off her warm body, knowing she would feel a brutal torrent of chilling air, which had slowly mounted through the night as the fire died in the wood-burning stove in the front room. That day the temperature couldn't stop her; she jumped out of bed, eager to get to school. There was a strange energy pumping through her that she had never felt before.

She suspected her ankle was better, but she was under strict orders to wear her blue nylon hooking boot. After a test walk across the bedroom floor, she found that she didn't need crutches. She was hoping her mom wouldn't notice they were missing.

Within minutes, she was ready for school. She headed down to the kitchen to fix her sisters some instant oatmeal.

The most delightful part of the morning for her was that she didn't have to report to her mom she had wet the bed.

I watched the two of them at a distance through the kitchen window.

"I thought I smelled oatmeal. Are your sisters up?" asked Bhren, entering the kitchen ready for work.

"Would you like a bowl, Mom?" asked Rhymee.

"No, but thanks," responded Bhren, watching Rhymee boiling water and grabbing bowls from the cabinet. "Where are your crutches?"

"My ankle feels better, Mom. I won't need to hobble on those things today. They only slow me down," said Rhymee, praying her mom would understand.

"Well, you may think you are well, but it has only been a week, Rhymee. A broken or fractured bone doesn't heal that quickly."

"This boot is pretty stiff, Mom. It seems to be doing the trick. I don't feel any pain."

"I just worry your ankle will heal wrong."

"Please don't make me use them, Mom. If I feel any pain at all, I'll grab them. I promise. Besides, I put most of my weight on the other foot."

"Oh, all right, but I don't like it," said Bhren.

"I'll go wake Rhondel and Rhegan," said Rhymee, adding a little extra sugar to the bowls.

"By the way, your hair is pretty tied back like that. There is something different about you today. Hmm…it must be that you have grown some. You're fifteen in a week. It seems like yesterday I was rocking you to sleep. I can't believe how time has flown by so quickly. Do you want to have company over for your birthday?"

I could feel Rhymee's nostalgia, and I saw flashes of images—Rhymee in her mother's lap during a rainstorm, the rain tapping on the windowpane. I felt her comfort and safety.

"Rhymee, did you hear me?" asked Bhren, noticing her daughter was daydreaming.

"Sorry, Mom. What?"

"Do you want to have a slumber party next week for your birthday?" asked Bhren more loudly this time.

Suddenly, I saw an image of Rhymee wetting the bed, and I felt her shame of the uncontrollable problem. It didn't take her long to answer her mom's question.

"No! I just want to rent some movies if that's okay."

"It's your birthday." Bhren sighed.

I was worried for Rhymee after biting her, so I followed her to school. After the bell rang and the students went inside, I quietly leapt to the school's wide, flat roof and listened.

Rhymee figured out early in the day she was unusually restless, and there was no cure for it. She tried socializing with her classmates between classes, but that was not helping. Several topics were of interest—the school dance, the new teacher, the book report due in Mrs. Lerry's class—but Rhymee was annoyed by the small talk. She wanted to leave, but she stayed. I was not only impressed by her politeness but also her steadfastness to suffer through things she did not enjoy.

She finished her homework during each class, thinking it would calm her nerves, but then she couldn't sit still. She was simultaneously thumping her leg and pencil.

"Miss Stewart, is something on your mind?" dryly asked Ms. Brighton, a substitute teacher in her third-period math class.

"No," Rhymee whispered. "I didn't realize I was being noisy."

"You are disturbing your classmates and me, so no more thumping."

"Yeah, Ms. Brighton's trying to read her romance novel," whispered a boy from behind Rhymee, softly chuckling.

"Do you have something to add, Mr. Smith?" asked Ms. Brighton.

"No, ma'am," he quickly answered.

"Good, now I expect quiet until the bell rings."

Athletics was worse. She had to sit out of the class because of her ankle. Normally she wouldn't have minded. She hated playing basketball, but today she needed to move, so gym was also torturous.

"Next week we will begin conditioning for track and field for the spring. Everyone will participate. We will be working out inside until it warms up a little," announced Mrs. Hastings, her coach and history teacher. "Break into your teams and warm up by doing free throws."

Rhymee watched her classmates play a game against each other. Team A squashed Team B, and by all the complaining from Team B, I assumed this was a normal occurrence. By the end of class, the girls were exhausted and pushed to their physical limits as they slowly made their way to the locker room to change. Rhymee sat on the gym's lowest bleachers, waiting on her two best friends, Holly and Laura. They were going to have lunch together.

"We missed you playing, Stewart. We get a kick out of your abilities," said Mary Snike, one of the girl's from Team A. She and her friend Jamie were the first two to exit after changing.

"Yeah, remember the last time she played? She scored points for our team on accident because she didn't understand the rules." Jamie Breddick laughed.

"Who could ever forget?" Mary laughed.

Normally Rhymee could suppress her emotions, but not today. My bite had changed her for good. She remembered one of her father's wise sayings.

She calmly quoted it under her breath. "If you don't take up for yourself, no one else will." She limped over and grabbed a lone basketball lying near the edge of the bleachers and threw it as hard as she could toward the basket. I heard it roll for a moment along the rim before it sank between the net. I laughed from the roof of the gym. *That will teach them*, I thought.

"Mary, you and Jamie best remember that I'll remain silent and observe unless I'm directly challenged, and then I'll prove that neither of you are any better than anyone else. We're all gifted. The difference between us is I don't want to show off. Now, excuse me," said Rhymee, hobbling away to join her friends.

The two girls silently stood there, dumfounded by what had just happened.

"Well put, my honorable lady!" I shouted as I leapt from the roof.

A few weeks later, Bhren drove Rhymee to Forrest Orthopedics for a checkup. I followed and sat in the waiting room next to an old woman. She cut her left eye toward me but then continued to read her magazine. Everyone else in the room ignored me. A long partition divided half the waiting room. Rhymee and Bhren sat on one side while I sat on the other.

"Mom, I need to go get a drink. I'll be back in a moment."

She knew I was there. I stood so I could circle the partition right when the nurse called her name.

"You can get a drink later. There's no time now," said Bhren, tossing her magazine aside.

I listened to her hobble down the tiled hallway and into a private room. Soon, the doctor thumbed through Rhymee's medical records attached to a clipboard then joined them.

"Have you been using your crutches?" Dr. Sayre asked before Rhymee had a chance to hobble up onto the examination table.

"Umm…most of the time," Rhymee lied.

"Most of the time or all the time? Remember my instructions? I did not want you to put weight on that foot. I hope we don't have to recast it," he said, expecting the worst while carefully detaching the boot.

Bhren sighed.

The doctor felt her ankle for quite some time, and then he ordered an X-ray.

"Rhymee, stay put. I will return shortly," said the doctor. "I need to speak to the radiologist."

Rhymee slightly smiled and nodded.

"I knew I should have made you use those crutches. Now you are going to have to wear a cast for twice as long," fumed Bhren after the doctor left the room.

"Mom, look at my foot. I know it's well," defended Rhymee.

"We'll see," said Bhren.

The doctor came back in holding a set of X-rays.

"Rhymee, I don't understand it, but X-rays don't lie. Your bone seems to have completely healed, but to be on the safe side, I want you to wear extra supportive shoes for at least a couple weeks," ordered Dr. Sayre.

"Thanks," said Rhymee, calmly smiling at her mom. She had known she was well for quite some time, but she was still excited she didn't have to wear the heavy, itchy boot any longer.

"Bhren, make sure she does as instructed," requested Dr Sayre.

"Oh, don't worry! I will!" replied Bhren.

On the way home, Rhymee quietly stared out the window. The pastures and treetops had begun to turn green. The day was warm with no wind. Early March in Arkansas meant there would be warm spring weather one day then possibly snow storms the next.

"Mom, can I stay outside for a while?" asked Rhymee, wanting to enjoy the sun while it lasted.

"I suppose, but no running! Understand?"

"I promise."

Rhymee was hanging her jacket on the knob of the front door when she noticed a six-foot frayed rope lying on the porch. Her dad must have left it there when he had come in earlier for lunch.

She picked up the rope and tested its strength. She then lugged it around the yard and house, trying to find a use for it. When her dog, Bandit, came around the corner, he stared at the rope for a moment then at Rhymee, seeming confused by its purpose.

"Come on, boy! Grab the rope!" said Rhymee, flinging one end of it like a striking snake.

Her malamute-elkhound mixed dog wasted no time in following Rhymee's request. He lunged at the other end of the rope, grabbed it in his jaws, and began to pull.

"Good boy! Let's play tug-of-war!" said Rhymee, pulling harder and harder.

Bandit would not let go, jerking the rope with his powerful neck and chops.

Rhymee began to laugh as she swayed backward at some points, trying to gain ground.

"This is the most fun I've had in a long time," she said.

"Rhymee, let him have the rope," I whispered, sensing the dog's agitation.

Rhymee heard me, but it was too late. Bandit bared his fangs and began growling. Rhymee realized her dog was not playing.

He pounced and in one bite ripped the flesh open on her arm from her elbow down to her wrist then continued to crunch into her skin through her sweater and undershirt. He would not let go long enough for Rhymee to make an escape.

"Bandit, stop!" she screamed, but the dog had snapped; his wild nature had taken over. The rope had become his enemy, and since Rhymee was holding the end of it, she had too.

I could not hypnotize animals as I could humans. Egan could, but I had not yet mastered that talent.

I couldn't let the dog get to her throat, so I decided to show myself for the first time. Exiting the barn in a hurry without my glasses, I was blinded by the sun; everything was distorted.

I was bewildered when Rhymee's emotions drowned my own out completely. The blindness I experienced was minor to Rhymee's pain that was being fueled by anger. It was when I felt a sudden vengeful courage that I knew she had no intention of running from the dog. Bandit had such a strong hold of her arm and had punctured deep holes in her skin, but I felt she no longer cared. Both of our worlds had grown foggy. She wrapped her hands around the dog's neck and smashed him to the ground then began strangling him.

"How dare you attack me, you stupid mutt!" she roared.

Bandit yipped, trying to gasp for air.

When Bhren came running out, I retreated back to my hiding place, impressed by Rhymee's aggressiveness.

"Rhymee, let him go!" sternly ordered Bhren, trying to figure out what had happened.

Rhymee hesitated in doing what she was told; adrenaline and pain were still surging through her body like electricity.

"What is going on?" asked Bhren in shock, noticing Rhymee's ripped clothing and bloody arm.

"Rhymee, you're killing him. Let him go," requested Bhren in a gentler voice, attempting to defuse the situation.

Rhymee finally responded to her mom's soothing tone. Bandit ran off as soon as she released her grip from his neck. She stood, taking deep breaths.

"What happened?" asked Bhren. "Did Bandit attack you?"

"He's not like Old Blue," cried Rhymee, finally allowing herself to feel the pain.

"No, I suppose he's not, but why did he come after you?" asked Bhren.

"We were playing tug-of-war. One moment he was playing, and then the next he was all over me."

"Why didn't you try to run?" asked Bhren, perplexed by her normally timid daughter's reaction.

"I couldn't break away!"

"You cannot play tug-of-war with that kind of dog!"

Rhymee just put her head down. "Am I grounded?"

Bhren did not answer her question. "We're going to have to find Bandit a new home. I knew better than to adopt him. He was the most aggressive, headstrong puppy of the litter. He has bit the propane man, one of my good friends, and now you. He has even threatened me! I wouldn't be surprised if your dad puts him down after this!"

"Please don't let Dad shoot him. It's my fault, and I feel bad about it now! You're right. I need to go find him and make up!"

"You need to leave him alone. I won't let your dad shoot him, but you and your sisters are to stay clear of him! There is no telling what he would have done to one of them, especially Rhegan. She could not have defended herself like you did! She is so small. He could kill her!"

"He could've killed me," Rhymee said under her breath.

"Go in the house so I can tend to your arm. We may have to make another trip to the ER for stitches, and I just bought that sweater! Now it's ruined!" said Bhren, confused about whom to be angrier with.

"Yes, Mother."

That night, while her family was enjoying television, Rhymee retreated to her room. She told everyone she wanted to read.

I watched Rhymee from the roof through the skylight.

For a long time she sat on her bed, rubbing her bandaged arm. Her feelings flowed through me like an emotional song. She was thinking of her dog. She felt horrible for what she had done to him and was worried about what he thought of her.

She stood up, pulled the curtain back, and stared out the window. Abruptly, I felt her thoughts change. She was focused on remembering my voice, warning her to stop the game. She wanted to know where it had come from or if it was her own conscience warning her. She was deep in thought when she noticed she was doing something she had been fearful of before: peering into the darkness. Her first reaction was to shut the curtain and run to the living room for safety, but something made her stay.

"Why have I been so afraid?" she asked herself.

Trying to find an excuse to go outside, she shoved on her new shoes and rushed down stairs to the kitchen. Her mother had forgotten to ask anyone to dump the garbage.

"Mom, Dad, I'm going to take out the garbage," said Rhymee, holding a plate of chicken bones and mashed potatoes.

"Okay," they both answered at the same time, still focused on their game show.

She stopped for a moment on the porch, peered through the darkness cautiously, and then slowly made her way to the weeds. For a long time, she stood there staring at the heavens. A newly found strength replaced her phobia of the dark, and she remembered the nights from long ago that were beautiful and inspired sweet dreams.

She looked around, searching for the cause of her terror but found nothing. She felt as if she could see more clearly and farther than ever before but blamed it on the bright, cloudless sky.

Taking a deep breath, she turned to go back in, but something stopped her. She took several more deep breaths and then sniffed the air.

"I can smell you now more than ever," she said, addressing me.

I was lurking in the forest, which lay beyond the field.

"You smell like a mixture of fresh tea grounds and maraschino cherries. Why do you leave for several days then return?" she asked, waiting for a response.

I have a smell? I asked myself, lifting my hand to my nose.

"You spoke to me today, didn't you?" asked Rhymee, pausing, hoping I would show myself.

I was mystified. I had never heard of humans possessing such a power. I wanted to speak to the elders about this, but I could not leave her long enough to do so.

"I'll not run or scream if you show yourself. I know you are powerful but mean me no harm," she explained. "It wasn't you I feared before; it was something else, but it's not here now," she said, looking up again to confirm her feelings.

I wanted to ask her what had caused her fright, but I held back. What if I terrified her? Humans looked upon our kind as monsters, and she already knew I was not human.

She stood there for a while longer.

"Rhymee, what are you doing? Get in here!" yelled Richard, stepping out to check on his daughter.

Rhymee sighed. "Sorry, Dad! I was looking at the stars."

"Well, that's a first," said Richard, surprised by his daughter's new behavior. "Please come in before you catch pneumonia!"

"Yes, sir!" said Rhymee.

When she reached the door, she stopped and turned back to my direction.

"Yep! I'm crazy!" she said to herself, speaking softly.

I laughed at her comment.

I was disturbed by the hold she had on me. I knew the end result. I would eventually lose her. She could not become a vampire. Was it because she was so different than any other human I had ever known, or was it the way she viewed her surroundings, or her innocence and love for her family and friends, or her unusual apprehensions? I could only guess the cause of my emotion, but at that moment, I loved nothing in the world more.

THE TRACK MEET

1987

Over the next few years, I became very competitive, but not with others. By age seventeen, I tried to best myself in everything I attempted. I kept the guise of being shy and awkward during school hours, even though I wasn't any longer. Upon reaching home, I would let my true nature show. My sisters and I would go exploring through the woods quite often. I'd gone from fearing the unknown to seeking it. I'd defend my sisters no matter the cost. On days when the woods held no interest, I'd throw my set of throwing knives into an old walnut tree over and over until I became an expert or shoot my lightweight bow at a paper target attached to a bale of hay. I took no interest in dressing up or wearing makeup and jewelry. I had no desire to pierce my ears, and a pair of faded denim jeans was always chosen over dresses and slacks. My close friends often complained that I was a tomboy because I wouldn't hang out with them and do girl things.

Rather than taking part in activities and discussions, I usually watched and took mental notes of how my classmates behaved, quietly determining that most teenage topics of conversation held no meaning for me.

I was made fun of on a regular basis by other students because I made myself an easy target, never saying anything in retaliation. I suppressed my anger and hatred by lowering my head and seeming defeated. I never forgot the wrongs others inflicted upon me or my friends, but I truly believed what went around would eventually come back around.

Track and field had become my favorite place at school. I didn't have to worry about fitting into any kind of a team, and I released a lot of my anger and stress through running. I'd not grown as tall as some of the girls, but I was strong-willed and had sturdy legs. My body did as my mind commanded.

It was the day of the district track meet. The athletes, both boys and girls, piled on the bus after school. I didn't like riding with this many people, especially in my track shorts. I was extremely self-conscious of the scars on my right knee and tried to hide them by keeping my gym bag draped over my leg.

"Aren't you excited?" asked Holly, one of my closest friends.

I was daydreaming and staring out the window, but I nodded.

"Do you think you'll beat your best time today?" asked Holly.

We each participated in different events. Holly was skilled in pole vault and hurdles, but she didn't like competing in long runs. I'd sometimes run the eight-eighty if the team was short a member. That was the only time I'd compete against Holly. I was not short, standing at five and half feet, but many of my classmates towered over me by several inches, including Holly. During a short sprint, the longer legged girls would always take the lead. I excelled in endurance running. I could run the mile in a little over four minutes.

I looked away from the window when I saw Coach Hastings making her way to the middle of the bus.

"Stewart, you will run the eight-eighty today along with Holly since Smith is out with the flu. Then you will have an hour or so before you have to run the two mile," ordered the coach, continuing her way to the back of the bus, giving instructions as she went.

"Great," I said.

"What's wrong?" asked Holly.

"You know I don't like the eight-eighty. It's over before it starts," I griped.

"You'll be okay. Just stay with me," said Holly.

"But you run faster than me," I said. I was somewhat nervous.

"I won't leave you," said Holly, trying to cheer me up.

"No, I want you to do your best. You deserve to letter. I don't want to hold you back. Why does she put me in situations where she knows I'll get made fun of?" I asked, feeling my coach was picking on me.

"Rhymee, you're a senior. Don't let it get to you. This is the last time we will get to compete, and if I hear anybody making fun of you, they'll answer to me!"

"Thanks, Holly," I said, turning my attention to the parking lot and gymnasium.

Slowly, a reddish-purple mist took form above the gym, floating there like a misshaped cloud. I unknowingly leaned into Holly and was pushing her out of the seat into the aisle.

"Rhymee, what are you doing?" asked Holly.

"Oh, sorry," I nervously responded, trying to pull my friend back up. "I just...umm...does it look like it's going to storm?"

Holly looked out the window and searched the sky for a moment, looking directly at the purplish mist.

"Uh, no, it's crystal clear. I watched the weather early this morning, and it isn't supposed to storm until the weekend. What gives you that idea anyway?"

"Oh, I thought it just looked a little hazy is all. Sorry I leaned on you. You know me and my daydreaming," I said.

I deliberately started a meaningless conversation about Holly's boyfriend, James, trying to ignore the cloud. The bus still had not pulled out, which was torturous. Why could I see and feel things others could not? Was it mental illness? I told myself the vile cloud was not real and that it was a figment of my crazy imagination. It had to be since no one else could see it.

It was five o'clock by the time we reached Harrison, and the sun was going down. I stepped off the bus and stretched along with the other team members. It had been a long, cramped ride.

"Everyone, warm up. You can go to the concession stand later! Sit in this section of bleachers!" ordered Coach Hastings, pointing to where she wanted everyone to stay grouped.

I followed Holly to the middle of the field and stretched. I sat down on the grass and began to touch my toes.

"Rhymee, what is wrong with you?" asked Holly. "It's not like you to keep your head pointed down. You've been doing that since we left."

"Nothing. I can look up! I just didn't realize I was doing that!" I said, hoping the cloud had not followed us.

"Are you sad about something?" asked Holly concerned. "Is it because I have a boyfriend and you don't? I'm sorry I ranted on about James so long."

I smiled and looked Holly in the eyes. "No, it's nothing like that. I'm happy for you."

"Okay, but promise to let me know if something is upsetting you?"

"I will."

I looked up expecting the worst, but the sky was clear. I knew the cloud was the same presence that had haunted me for years, but I didn't understand why I could suddenly see it. During my childhood, I could feel a strange atmosphere around my house and in the woods. Sometimes it was inviting and made me feel safe while other times my instincts told me to dread whatever it was. Through the years, my fear slowly turned to anger. I wanted rid of it. *I'm becoming sicker*, I thought. *What to do?* I wanted to tell someone what I was witnessing—my parents, my friends, my sisters—but I knew I couldn't. They'd think I was nuts. I had to deal with this problem on my own.

It was a good thing I was at a track meet. I needed to run so I could de-stress.

While running the two mile, I heard a sultry male voice say to try harder, to run faster. It was the same voice that had warned me about my dog, Bandit. He was encouraging me. So far he'd given me good advice, so I found myself wanting to trust him. I became overly excited when I heard him. I knew he was watching me from somewhere in the bleachers. I wanted to show him my strength, so I pushed myself harder than ever before in the race.

I was the last to board the bus. I searched the area, trying to catch a glimpse of the man that spoke to me with his mind. *Who is he? Maybe he is my fairy godfather. Huh…like I believe that.* The answer hit me; he was my guardian angel. That was why he watched out for me. *There can be no other reason*, I thought.

Mom was waiting patiently for me in the car at the gymnasium. It was 12:30 a.m., and she was yawning uncontrollably.

I was worried about the cloud and staring at the gym like it was some kind of monster. I wasn't paying attention and almost tripped over a parking block.

Some of the students began to chuckle.

"Are you okay, Rhymee?" asked Holly. I could tell she was trying not to laugh along with the others.

"Just great!" I answered, finally spotting my mom in the distance. "See you Monday!"

Mom tried to act like she hadn't seen me trip. She stepped out of the car in her bathrobe. "Have a good time, sweetie?"

"Mom, you aren't dressed?" I said, quickly jumping in the passenger's seat, hoping none of my classmates had seen.

"I have my flannels on under this. Besides, what do you expect at this hour?" she answered.

"You're right. Thanks for picking me up. Sorry I kept you up so late," I said. I desired the comfort of my own pajamas.

"How did you perform?"

"Okay I suppose. I'm really just sleepy, looking forward to bed. It's been a long day."

"It has been for me too. I don't want to go to work tomorrow. I hit my thumb hard today hammering caps on motors. I'm sure it will feel worse in the morning." Mom sighed, checking her tightly wrapped bandage. "Promise me you will finish college and get a good job so that you don't have to work like I do."

"Did you cut it?" I asked, concerned. I wished I could give my parents the world. I loved them so much.

"I hit it so hard that my nail began to bleed."

"Mom, you have got to be more careful!" I felt her pain.

"Just promise me, Rhymee!"

"I promise but not because I fear working. I don't want to disappoint you or Dad!"

"You could never disappoint us, Rhymee."

I began to answer her with shorter and shorter responses the closer we got to home. My mind again drifted to the voice I had heard at the track meet.

"Rhymee, you seem distracted, more so than usual. What's bothering you?"

I didn't answer. I didn't want to talk to her about it.

"Rhymee…"

"Sorry, Mom, I'm just tired. I don't mean to ignore you."

"Well, make sure you go straight to bed when we get in."

"I will." I was ready to sleep soundly, without nightmares. Maybe my guardian would keep them away.

RHYMEE'S DREAM

1987

I had followed Rhymee to the track meet, but when it was over, I came back to the farm and waited anxiously. I was relieved when she got home. Through our connection, I had encouraged her to run her best.

She leapt out of the car and quickly crept up the stairs.

"Good night. Don't forget your prayers," said Bhren, heading to her room.

"Okay, Love you, Mom," responded Rhymee.

It was little conversations like this that made me love not only Rhymee but her entire family. I would defend any of them to the death. I could feel Rhymee's devotion toward them, which made me insanely protective. It would have killed her if something bad happened to her family, and it would have destroyed me to see Rhymee in pain.

I could hear her throw on her nightshirt. I waited until she was finished, and then I jumped to the roof to watch from the skylight. She checked to see if her sisters were soundly sleeping.

"My friend, if you are out there, please talk to me! I fear I'm going crazy," she whispered into the windowpane, expecting no response.

At first, I hesitated but then thought, *Why not? I have spoken to her before.* Now she was old enough to understand I was not a figment of her imagination. I jumped from the roof and hid behind a tree.

"You are not crazy," I softly responded. "What troubles you?"

Stunned by my response, she jumped backward and began rubbing her arms, vigorously trying to calm her nerves.

"Well, go on," I politely requested.

"I…umm…who or what are you?" asked Rhymee quietly.

"There is much to explain, and I will tell as much as I know, but the hour is late. I know you need to rest. Does something else trouble you this night?"

"No," she fibbed, suddenly feeling awkward. "When can we talk?"

"Tomorrow, when everyone sleeps, but you need to stay inside in case your parents wake. I suggest you walk downstairs to the front room so you do not disturb your sisters."

"Do you promise?"

"I always keep my word, Rhymee, but I fear once you discover what I am, you will detest me."

"I doubt that. You've been around us for years and have never offered to hurt anyone."

"How do you know?" I asked.

Rhymee didn't answer my question. For a moment, she began doubting my nature and intentions.

"I…really…don't… Are you an angel?"

I laughed. "No, Rhymee, but I would never hurt you or your family. Our conversation must wait until tomorrow night. I have been silent for many years. Both of us need to practice patience," I explained, just as eager to speak to her, but daybreak approached. She had many questions, and so did I. Unfortunately, our discussion that night had to end as quickly as it had begun.

"Tomorrow night then! Good night…whoever you are."

"Goodnight, Rhymee."

After she was deep in sleep, I made my way to the well. I closed my eyes and connected my mind to hers. She was vividly dreaming. This was what I saw through her eyes:

A red cloud took on a cylindrical form and traveled close to the ground with great speed until it reached an old, rotted, hollow tree stump in the middle of a meadow several hundred miles from the Stewarts' farm. Changing its form at the head to the shape of a church key, it dove into the stump. From there, it pressed with ease through several layers of rock and soil. It stopped when it reached a spacious underground cave, glowing fiery red.

Upon reaching her destination, the wraith restructured its misty essence back to a pear shape and formed gigantic wings along with muscular, long arms and legs. Large, bony spikes protruded from its calves and elbows and acted as heels to help give it support.

There were a total of six wraiths in the cave, but the other five did not hold any particular shape.

"Ah, you have returned, Lurhide. What news?" asked one of the creatures.

"Grave, Salumus," answered the one called Lurhide, perching on a nearby boulder, tapping her whiplike, middle claw, which seemed to contain twenty or more joints. Her other four claws were on average three inches in length.

Rhymee woke, and I came out of the nightmare with her. I leapt to the roof so I could check on her. She was sweating from what she witnessed, but she had gone back to sleep. Was her dream a figment of her imagination, or were those creatures real? I remembered Egan's story from long ago. He had said a mercuride, known as Salumus, haunted him. Was this the same creature? Rhymee was able to detect magical beings and events that most other humans could not. Was that why these creatures watched her? Maybe they were hoping she could help them since they knew she could see them.

I recognized the tree stump and meadow from her vision. I had passed through there many times when hunting. Maybe Rhymee had seen the area before so it was just a place for her dream to occur. I doubted it. Were these wraiths there conversing in an underground cavern at this moment?

Egan feared these creatures, even after he became vampire, so I was apprehensive, but I had to know. I stared at her for a moment longer, trying to muster my courage, and then I jumped down and ran wholeheartedly toward the meadow.

EAVESDROPPING

How could Rhymee dream about a real place and events? I asked myself, dashing through the forest. Had my bite given her the ability? Once I reached the edge of the forest, I stopped. If these creatures were real, I did not want them to hear me. I surveyed the area and discovered the mossy stump. Its hollow center and sprigs darting upward looked the same as in her dream. I noiselessly crept to the stump and rested my head against it. When I heard a discussion taking place, I jerked my head away, startled. Once my suspicion was confirmed, my first instinct was to run from the place, but curiosity got the best of me. I forced myself to stay and listen, so I again rested my ear against the damp, dead wood.

"Stay hidden and keep your distance from this Rhymee. Now that she knows we are real, she needs to forget us, place us in her past. Can you do as you are told?" asked one of the wraiths.

"You talk to me as if I am stupid. I will handle this as I see fit."

"Are you going to let her talk to you that way, my lord?" one of them asked. "We would have been hung by our talons and whipped for such insubordination."

"I shall get her when she least expects it," answered their leader vengefully.

"None of us respect you anymore, Lurhide!" added another one.

"Enough, I do not like this news, but it is nothing we cannot overcome," one of them said authoritatively.

Overcome what? I wondered. I assumed he was Salumus.

"I will hide my anger and beg forgiveness from those who bar our way to the realm of Lethun. Shurkhon, you are in charge while I am gone. Remain here so the others may report to you."

"As you wish," replied the one called Shurkhon.

"Lurhide, you know your orders."

"Why can't I return with you?" asked Lurhide defiantly. "Have Shurkhon stay to watch the girl!"

Fury engulfed my senses. I knew they were talking about Rhymee.

"What can I say? I tire of you, Lurhide! You are a nagging pest! Does that sum it up for you?"

"Make no mistake, I feel the same! I only wish to see Lethun once more. I cannot understand why I followed you to this place called earth! I lost my beautiful body because of the likes of you!"

"You stinking…"

Lurhide laughed hard at Salumus. "What are you going to do? Kill me?"

"Lurhide, you best remember my retribution is like no other. If I have to wait a century to punish you for your foul mouth, be assured I will."

"There is no punishment any worse than this. I will do as you wish, but for my own reasons, not yours. We are all powerless here! Our plans always fail!" shouted Lurhide.

So they are powerless, I thought. I was a little relieved for Rhymee's sake, but I still hated the fact that these creatures were tormenting her. I had to find a way to end it. I wanted to see her happily living in peace.

"Silence!" shouted Salumus, causing stalactites, medium-sized rocks, and pieces of the cave's roof to crash to the ground. The only noise in the cave for several moments was trickling water pooling up on the floor of a large limestone basin. That was my signal to leave. I quietly snuck out of the meadow then rushed back to the farm.

When I think back on it, I was foolish to believe the mercurides were helpless. I left the most precious thing in the world vulnerable to attack.

CONVERSATION IN THE NIGHT

When it was time to talk the next night, Rhymee stealthily and swiftly made her way down the stairs. As she stood at the window, I could hear her heart racing.

"Are you out there?" she asked softly.

"I am."

"May I know your name?" she asked.

"Thadacus Enman Goodridge," I answered.

"Can I ask you something without you becoming offended?"

"Go for it," I replied.

"What are you, Thadacus? I know you're not human."

"You will not like the answer to that question. I am definitely not an angel," I warned her.

"You won't scare me. I know you've been around for as long as I can remember. I thought I was going crazy at times because I could feel you watching, so please tell me."

"Most fear us. We have a bad reputation among your kind."

"Why?" asked Rhymee.

"I kill without remorse. I feed upon the ones who should not have been born."

Rhymee began to pace back and forth. I had upset her. Maybe talking to her had been a mistake. She did not understand my nature.

"By the ones who should not have been born… What do you mean?"

"I kill murderers, rapists, thieves, and an assortment of others. Do you fear me?" I had to ask. I didn't know how I could go on if the girl I had come to love hated me.

She was quiet.

"You do not need to respond. I know the answer." I was thinking about my cave. I did not want to go back there…alone.

"No, I was thinking of myself and doubting my own goodness. I've stolen things and have not always done the right thing. Why haven't you killed me?" asked Rhymee, remembering the track meet and how she wanted to teach Bonnie, the girl from Garland High, a lesson. "I judge others, and I know I shouldn't. There's a rage within me. Sometimes it consumes me. When that happens, I can't see anything but fog. I suppose, in my own way, I'm just as bad as the others."

"Rhymee, don't even classify yourself with them. I would never harm a child. Children do bad things—that is why they have parents. You could not have asked for a better set. Your entire family is gifted with purpose. They each bring unique gifts to this world, but you are like no other I have ever met."

"But, Thadacus, I'm not a child any longer, yet I still make mistakes. I do things against my better judgment quite often."

"Okay, you are making me feel guilty for killing corrupted individuals. I knew a conversation with you would be an interesting one."

"Oh, sorry! I didn't mean to make you feel bad."

"I know that about you," I replied.

"Thadacus, why must you hunt? Aren't you in danger of being injured or killed?"

I laughed.

"What are you?" she asked, wanting a straight answer.

"I am a vampire," I said, expecting to startle her. "I must feed upon blood to survive. Now you fear me, don't you?"

She thought for a moment before responding.

"No, not necessarily. Many creatures created by God are nourished by blood. They aren't evil. They serve a purpose. To kill without cause for the sake of killing is evil."

"Do you fear me a little?" I asked. I could feel her emotions, so I could tell she was scared.

"I'd be lying if I said no. I have a great respect for what you are, but I'm in shock more than anything else by your very existence."

For a moment, there was an awkward silence, but she soon thought of another question.

"Is that why you leave for days at a time? You're searching for food?"

"Yes. I don't like it."

"You don't like hunting?" asked Rhymee. "I'm confused because earlier you said you hunted without remorse."

"I do not like leaving you," I said frankly.

Rhymee tried to control her emotion. She didn't want me to know she was slightly embarrassed and happy that I was finally speaking to her and that I had protected her through the years and that she hated it when I was away. She tried to cover her feelings with another question, but I knew how she felt. The feelings that overwhelmed her were flooding my mind. It was hard to separate her feelings from mine.

"Of all the places in the world, why do you stay here?" she asked.

I was quiet, trying to think of the right response. I knew the answer; she was more precious to me than anything else the world had to offer. When I thought of how much I loved her, I felt woozy. It was like sucking on a hard piece of candy, knowing it would eventually wither away to nothing. My will of remaining alone so that I would not again feel the pain of loss gave into my heart's desire to stay with her.

"I have lived all over the world and have seen many sights. Northwest Arkansas is one of the most beautiful. Never take it for granted you live in such a place. You are one of the lucky ones," I answered.

"Is that the only reason?" she shyly asked.

"You already know it is not," I replied, saying nothing more.

"Why am I so different?" she asked, not believing she was anything special.

"Well, you are offhandedly talking to me, a vampire, like it is some everyday occurrence." I laughed. "I have never met anyone who sees this world as you do. You feel the magic of the earth and appreciate nature and its magnificence. Technology and science have made most humans blind."

"But there are others who see and appreciate nature. There are earth activists, animal conservationists, and botanists trying to save trees. I even see witches occasionally holding meetings in Trilson Park. What is it about me?"

"Do you want to join their cause?" I asked amused.

"No!" she quickly answered.

"Why?" I asked.

"I'm not a follower. As far as the witches go, I fear for them. They are meddling in things they should not and are trying to gain power over something they do not understand."

"Do you understand?" I quickly interjected.

"No, and I don't want to. I know something more is out there, something that holds great power and is dangerous. Are you from that place, Thadacus?"

I avoided discussing what I had seen in her nightmare. I could not bear to bring up that memory or that I had the ability to experience her dreams. I felt guilty for invading her privacy, but I couldn't help it. It had been necessary to protect her.

"I was the last one to become vampire, but I do not remember what that entailed. I was once human. I know very little about my kind. A powerful magic turns us to what we are. There can only be so many of us because we are immortal."

"May I ask how old you are?"

"Let's put it this way. If I were still human, I would be disgustingly decrepit, like a shriveled up zombie," I joked, trying to lighten the mood.

She giggled. "I wonder what my friends or parents would think of you—not that I would ever tell anyone. You can trust me, Thadacus. It's just that…well, it's good to know I'm not crazy."

"You are far from it, and I know I can trust you, Rhymee."

I was quiet for a moment, deep in thought. I was enjoying the moment so much that sadness crept into my soul. I didn't want this happy time in my life to end, even though I knew it must.

"Thadacus, are you still out there?" she asked, sounding worried I had left.

"Yes, but it is late. You need to wake early in the morning. We will talk some more tomorrow. Please get some rest," I requested, saddened by the thought of her dying, but I could never ask a vampire to die in her stead.

"I'm sorry if I'm keeping you from something."

"You're not, but I must insist that you sleep. Otherwise, you won't function properly tomorrow."

"I couldn't sleep if I wanted to. I'll just think of you all night," she admitted.

"You might surprise yourself. I know what's best for you. I'm your elder, remember."

"I was raised to respect my elders. I'll do as you have requested, but I fear going to sleep."

"Why?" I asked.

"I fear you will not speak to me again, that this has been a dream."

"I promise I will speak to you on a regular basis, except when I hunt."

"Good night then, my friend," she said.

"Sleep soundly," I said, grieving deeply over the thought of losing her eventually but hiding the fact.

The next day, I followed Rhymee to school and listened from a sheltered spot on the roof. She could not concentrate during most of her classes. Her thoughts constantly drifted to me. She was able to halfway listen in literature class because her teacher was discussing a topic that grabbed her interest: the codes of a knight. I remembered her and Rhondel a few years back pulling the ends of their mom's flyswatters off and using the wired handles as swords. They lunged and parried at each other furiously until the tip of Rhondel's weapon slashed a deep cut in Rhymee's chest. Rhondel's eyes widened. "I'm sorry, Rhymee. It was an accident."

Rhymee took a few deep breaths and held her cut for a moment. "I know. I won't tell Mom, but we should stop." The ideas of chivalry brought that fond memory to my mind.

"Can anyone tell us what these codes are?" asked Mrs. Lerry. A kid named John answered the teacher: "Loyalty, generosity, honesty, showing courtesy to women, and defending the weak and less fortunate." I found Rhymee's interest in this subject ironic. Even though we were born in different time periods, we both craved to know everything regarding the Middle Ages.

"Ms. Stewart, I want to hear your thoughts," asked Mrs. Lerry.

Rhymee felt like speaking up for once. After all, she was about to graduate.

"I'll live my life by those basic rules, as should all of you," said Rhymee, boldly speaking her mind.

"Really? What is your favorite from the list?" asked Mrs. Lerry, amazed she had been wrong about Rhymee paying attention.

"That's easy. Shunning unkindness, treachery, and unjust actions—you know, like making fun of others for pleasure," she said, staring coldly at one classmate in particular.

Daralee Brown had made fun of Rhymee on numerous occasions, but that was the first time Rhymee had said anything in defense. Daralee put her head down in shame.

"Interesting…and what were these codes defining?" asked Mrs. Lerry, searching the room for other daydreamers or sleepers.

Rhymee slowly sank back into her seat. *Good, maybe Daralee will leave me alone*, she thought.

Rhymee dashed off the bus and sought solitude.

"Rhondel, go do the dishes. Mom's orders. Rhegan, go clean your bedroom," she said, wanting rid of her sisters for a while.

"No!" said Rhondel. "I'm coming with you. I know you're up to something."

"Rhondel, I swear! When are you going to start acting like an adult? Come on. I will help you with the dishes," said Rhymee, giving up on speaking to me for the moment.

"I will talk to you later, Rhymee," I whispered.

Rhymee stopped for a moment and smiled. I knew she had heard me.

"What's going on?" asked Rhondel, noticing her sister's odd behavior. "Do you have a new boyfriend?"

"Wouldn't you like to know?" said Rhymee, following Rhondel into the house and playfully scrubbing her head.

Rhymee watched the five o'clock news with her family. There had been a prison break. The escapee had raped and murdered a child a few years before. Although Cummins was several hours from Prairie Grove, according to the news, the criminal was suspected to be heading north in their direction.

"Girls, homework!" ordered Bhren. "Hop to it!"

Rhymee finally found her opportunity to sneak upstairs. Her parents no longer checked to see if she had homework. She was about to graduate and had earned her parents' trust with good grades. She was a straight-A student.

"You don't have to worry about the prisoner. I need to hunt anyway, so I can't stay long tonight," I said, standing from behind the barn.

Rhymee was a little disappointed but at the same time wanted me to hunt after hearing what the man had done.

"I understand," she said. "Please be careful."

I laughed.

"What's funny?"

"You're telling me to be careful, and I am virtually invincible."

"What about wooden stakes through your heart or fire or getting beheaded or getting trapped in sunlight? None of that holds any truth?" asked Rhymee, reflecting on all the vampire movies she had seen where the vampire's skin turned to ash at the slightest touch from the sun.

"None of it. Our bones, tendons, and ligaments are harder and stronger than any known substance on earth. A blade couldn't sever or break them. I am blind in daylight. It is kind of the same difference as night for you—minus the moon and stars. I can see images of things, but not well."

"Where do you go at daybreak?" asked Rhymee.

"Any place providing solitude works. I have spent many days in the old well near the barn. Your sisters are coming, and

I need to go. I suspect I will not be gone but a night. This one is close. Take care while I am away."

"Thadacus, I'll miss you. I don't feel the same when you leave."

"I will miss you too!"

"I…never mind," said Rhymee.

"What is it?"

"May I see you sometime?"

"If everything permits, I will meet you tomorrow night at the pond near the farm."

"What do you look like?" she asked, trying to form a picture of me in her mind.

"You'll soon find out. Here they come."

"Who are you talking to?" asked Rhondel, entering the room suddenly.

"No one, just myself…practicing a speech," said Rhymee, annoyed.

I lingered a moment longer and listened to the three of them.

"Rhymee, read me a story," Rhegan requested. "I know Rhondel won't."

Rhymee looked at her little sister and suddenly thought of the little girl who had lost her life to the killer, and anger swelled in her gut at the thoughts of someone hurting either of her sisters. She read to Rhegan, and even Rhondel snuggled up and fell asleep next to her big sister.

For a moment, the icy hunger overwhelming my body was stifled, and I felt warm at the thought of Rhymee's ability to nurture. I loved her sisters in much the same way, like a brother. Rhymee will make a good mother, I thought. I had not reflected on the fact that she may want to be a mom someday, but I could never have children. That part of the vampire's myth was true. Our magical bodies were barren. Our organs became permanently suspended. My cold hunger came back as I became glum. Could I let another man touch her? I think I'd die inside. I felt vulnerable; my fate was in her hands. Why was I thinking about it? Rhymee was young—too young to have children any time soon. I decided to enjoy the present and deal with the future when it came time.

MEETING

At sundown the next evening, Rhymee cautiously walked toward the scum-coated pond located a quarter mile from the farm. I stood at the small wooden dock, which stretched out to the center of the water. I watched Rhymee make her way toward me.

She appeared older than she was. At seventeen and a half, she had grown into a stunning, young woman. She was luminescent in the twilight, like a pixie. Reflecting back, I was naive for not realizing the true cause of those changes. I assumed it was love's influence.

It was quiet, except for the occasional splash caused from a turtle jumping off a log into the water. I was nervous and anxious in anticipation. What would she think of me?

After fighting her way through thick greenbriers, stinging nettles, and a myriad of other wild plants on the rarely used trail, Rhymee reached the rim of the pond.

She suddenly noticed my silhouette, and she jumped. She thought I would be hiding from her view.

"Thadacus?" she asked in a cautious voice, waiting for an answer and ready to run if I didn't confirm her question.

"Rhymee, it is I. Do not fear me," I said tenderly.

After hearing my voice, she did not hesitate in making her way to the rickety dock where I stood waiting.

"I am sorry you had to struggle through weeds and brambles to reach me, but I felt this spot would provide the most solitude," I began, trying to ease her nerves and mine.

"That's okay! I've walked that trail many times but obviously not enough lately," she said, staring at me intently in the moonlight while pulling cockleburs from her tangled hair.

"Did you catch the prisoner?" she asked.

"I tracked him for a while last night. I know where he is hiding. I will go there again tonight and make my move when the time is right."

"Oh, good luck then."

"Do I look like a monster?" I asked, changing the subject. I did not want to think about feeding. I attempted to sound bold rather than nervous.

She didn't answer quickly. Instead, she studied my eyes.

"You look younger than I thought you would. By the moonlight, you appear to be in your early thirties, and your eyes are like nothing I've ever seen. The most shocking thing is you look like a normal human, save your eyes. They are glowing," replied Rhymee.

"I am consumed with magic, Rhymee. No part of me is human any longer, save my conscience and memories."

"You don't appear to have fangs either."

"Oh, make no mistake, I have them. It takes a well-trained eye to see the small holes at the ends of my eyeteeth, which hold my retractable fangs. I don't really have the ability to show them right now. They seem to have a mind of their own. They usually appear when I feel certain emotions, like anger, sadness, or satisfaction."

"What other magical powers do you have besides being immortal?"

"I can see better and farther than any human at night. For example, I can see every shade of color in your eyes, which come together to form an army-jacket green. Your skin is pale white touched by a few freckles, and right now you are somewhat chilly because you have goose bumps forming on your arms. I can see the same colors at night as you see in the day. I can hear things at a great distance and can run fast without ever tiring."

Rhymee stepped back and turned her back to me.

"What is it?" I asked concerned.

"I just…well, I…" she hesitated.

"Rhymee, you can tell me anything or ask me anything. You cannot offend me."

"I doubt my own sanity. I feel like I'm in a dream. How could such a beautiful, powerful creature take interest in me? There are so many humans. I know I lack self-esteem. I'm recognizing that fact this very moment, but I don't deserve such a gift. I'm not any different than any other human," she reasoned.

"But in my eyes, you are different," I defended, attempting to make her understand.

"How am I so different?" she asked.

"Maybe you are not so different to others, but I view you as quite unique, and I love everything about you," I blurted out, not meaning to.

She whirled around quickly. A sudden surge of guilt overwhelmed her.

"Thad, I have to go. I shouldn't have come out here. I'm sorry!" she yelled, rushing back up the trail, ignoring the weeds cutting her arms and cheeks.

I did not try to stop her. I should not have told her that I loved her. I scared her away by saying it. What was I thinking? She was too young.

I stood there a long time, regretting that I had agreed to meet her. I should have just continued to talk to her from a distance. My limbs all the way to my fingertips and toes grew icy cold. I welcomed the feeling. I wanted my heart to freeze along with the rest of my body. I didn't want to feel her guilt or my pain.

"You are hungry. You need to feed," a light, radiant voice suggested.

I veered around, seeking its source, but saw or smelled nothing that could have caused it.

What the…? Now I am going mad, I thought, but the voice was right. The ice shooting through my limbs was hunger. Maybe it was my subconscious mind speaking. I wanted to run and hunt, so I had no problems listening and following the advice.

CONFUSED

My parents would not approve. Why had I agreed to meet a vampire of all things? What was I thinking? He could have put some kind of seductive, vampiric spell on me. Maybe he had been for years. Was that why I was attracted to him? I had never felt like this toward anyone, ever. I wanted to do the right thing. Was I intimidated by our age difference or his wisdom? I felt so confused.

I took a deep breath as I stepped inside the front door. I was trying not to cry. My mom was sitting on the couch. She had been waiting for me.

"Rhymee, where have you been? I needed you earlier and couldn't find you."

"I just took a walk. I needed some fresh air."

"At this hour? I don't like you out at this time of evening by yourself. Your dad spotted a mountain lion the other day. You could be attacked. You couldn't defend yourself if that happened."

I sighed. "What did you need help with?"

"Your aunt Hada is holding a yard sale in town. She asked if we had anything that we wanted to add. I was hoping you could go through your old clothes and pull out the items you don't wear and gather anything else you want rid of. It's a good opportunity for you to earn some extra cash."

"Yeah…I'll go do it right now," I said. It was my opportunity to go to my room. I hoped my sisters were still at the kitchen table doing their homework. I needed to cry, and I didn't want any of them to see.

"Are you all right, honey? You seem upset."

"Yeah, I'm good," I lied.

I quickly climbed the stairs. When I reached my room, I locked the door. I was relieved to find I was alone. I began to cry as I opened the closet door. I pulled out piles of old clothes, but I could only think about him. Why had I run from him? He hadn't put a spell on me. I was stupid for thinking it. I remembered when he left the last time, and I grew weak with the fear. Would he leave again because of my childish behavior? I paced back and forth and began to tingle and itch.

"That's just great…hives on top of everything else!"

I heard a soft knock at the door. "Rhymee, I know you haven't had dinner, so I brought you up a plate. We ate fried chicken. It's still warm," said Mom.

I quickly wiped my face, but it was too late. I looked like a raccoon with a red mask. I couldn't do anything but open the door. I tried to think of an excuse for my tears. I was blank. What could I say?

"Honey…"

"Hold on, Mom. I'm coming."

I turned to the closet as she came in and started folding an old blouse.

"Here, honey. Where do you want this?"

"The nightstand's fine," I said, trying to sound normal.

She immediately knew I had been crying. "Rhymee, turn around."

I slowly did as she said. "I…"

"What is the matter, honey? Talk to me."

"It's no big deal," I lied.

"It has to be, or you wouldn't be crying. You can tell me anything. I will understand. Did your sisters do something?"

"No…"

"Then what?"

"It's just that I feel like I have done something wrong," I said, leaving out the details.

"What?" she asked. I could tell my mom was alarmed, but she tried to hide the fact and listen to me.

I hesitated to answer. I was trying to find the right words. "It's boy trouble."

"I didn't know you liked a boy. You haven't mentioned him before. What grade is he in?"

I put my head down. A tear rolled down my cheek. "It doesn't matter."

"Oh, honey, I should not have asked that. What happened to upset you like this?"

"After the way I treated him, I don't think he will want to hang out with me anymore."

"Relationships can be confusing. You're only seventeen, Rhymee. It's okay to be confused. Anyway, I'm sure he's just as confused as you are."

I doubt it, I thought. Again I was reminded of Thad's age and wisdom.

"Rhymee, if he cares for you at all, he will try to work through things. He won't abandon you because of a disagreement, and if he does leave you, he's not worthy of you. You are a beautiful, caring, and smart girl. The right person will come along."

But he's not like anyone else, I thought. "Thanks, Mom. That makes me feel a little better."

"May I ask what he did?"

"He didn't do anything. I pushed him away because I thought that you all would be upset that I have a boyfriend," I said.

"Rhymee, I would become worried if you didn't eventually find a boyfriend. It's normal for a girl your age to take interest in someone, but you shouldn't become serious until you are older. We've already talked about that though. You know your dad's rule—he needs to meet your boyfriend."

"Don't worry, Mom. I'm just trying to get to know him. There is nothing wrong with that, right?"

"Not a thing."

"And I remember Dad's rule." *In a way, I have already broken it*, I thought.

"Good! Now, dry up your tears. You're going to be all right," she said, hugging me tightly.

"Okay, thanks for talking to me, Mom."

"You're welcome. Now, I need to go finish a load of laundry," she said, leaving my room. "You can work on the closet tomorrow."

I fell back on the bed. I was still sad, but I felt better. Mom was right. I could care for Thad without becoming too serious. I remembered him telling me that he trusted me. It was my turn. I had to trust him. What was wrong with meeting him and just talking? There was nothing wrong with that. He hadn't tried to hurt me in any way. He had protected me and my family for years. He didn't even chase after me when I ran from him. I took a deep breath. I wanted him to come back. Could he hear my thoughts? I hoped so. I concentrated. *I miss you and need you. Please talk to me*, I thought, but I was interrupted.

My sisters entered the room.

"What's wrong, Rhymee?" asked Rhegan.

"Yeah…I can see you've been crying," said Rhondel.

It's times like this that I need my own room, I thought. "Go ask Mom, if you must know. I have already talked to her," I said. I knew that would shut them up.

They looked at me awkwardly then climbed into bed.

"Sorry. I was just worried," snapped Rhondel.

"Yeah, Rhymee!" said Rhegan.

"I'm sorry. I just need some sleep," I apologized.

"Fine," said Rhondel.

I again concentrated on Thad, but he didn't talk to me that night.

EXPLANATIONS

As I was hunting, I heard her call to me. My hunger could not be ignored, so I pressed on through the night, searching for the prisoner. I didn't know if I should speak to her after intimidating her like I had. Maybe it was better to just leave her alone. She was right to be scared of me. She was right to worry about what her family would think.

I watched the convict for four nights before I feasted. I had to wait until he was alone. As the blood meal warmed my insides, I came to my senses and felt Rhymee's sorrow. I didn't hesitate to return back to the farm.

She stepped out on the porch, alone at dusk, and stared aimlessly through the darkness.

"Thad, I'm sorry. Please talk to me. I shouldn't have run off. I won't do it again. Please don't leave me. I was just mixed up," she said softly. I could smell the salty tears falling from her face.

"Rhymee, don't cry. You haven't done anything wrong. I was only away because I had to hunt."

"Thad, I just—"

"Rhymee, you don't need to explain," I said.

"Yes, I do. I want you to know that it makes me happy that you love me and that you have been here for a long time so I can understand why you love me. I think you are a beautiful, powerful, and wise being. It's just that I don't really know you. Please don't take that statement the wrong way. I want to know you. I want that more than anything else in the world."

She paused and took a deep breath.

"Rhymee…" I tried to cut her off so I could explain my behavior.

"I thought you left again," she choked.

"I would not leave you over something so trivial. Rhymee, I won't desert you ever unless you ask me to."

"Good…because I don't want you to ever leave me."

"You don't have to love me, Rhymee, but I will love you no matter what, and I will never ask anything from you in return. If you need me for anything, all you have to do is ask, and it shall be done."

"Can we start out by talking and go from there? I probably sound silly compared to the people you have met in your lifetime," she said shyly.

"On the contrary, I have met many idiots in my time. It is a rare occasion to meet anyone with any sense."

Rhymee giggled, and I could feel her spirits lift. "Where are you?" she asked.

I stepped from behind a thick tree trunk.

"May I come to you?"

"Please."

She slowly walked toward me. "I want to be close to you when I tell you this."

"Go on," I whispered.

"I trust you, Thad. May I touch your hand?"

"I don't know what will happen. I have never let a human touch me, less I was involved in a heated battle," I explained, slowly stretching out my hand.

Rhymee cautiously touched the top of my hand with her index finger.

"Ouch!" she exclaimed, quickly pulling back.

"What happened?" I asked.

"It was like touching an electrified fence!"

"I am sorry, Rhymee. I didn't mean to hurt you."

"I'm okay, just a little startled is all," she said, massaging her finger. "After all, it was worth it. I feel reenergized."

"Rhymee, a long time ago, you spoke to me. Your foot was injured, remember? I wasn't ready to speak to you back then, but how did you know I was there?" I asked, wanting to know the answer to that mystery.

"I noticed throughout the years a change in the air from time to time. The aroma would come and go, and I knew it was not caused by a change in season. You have a very unique fragrance that drifts lightly across the breeze."

"Blood and carnage?" I interrupted.

She giggled.

"No, nothing like that."

"I still don't know how you can detect all that. It is intriguing. The rest of your family has not identified my unusual odor."

"Maybe it's because they don't seek the extraordinary magical things living among us. Although, I must admit I'm still in shock myself."

"Shhh," I requested.

Rhymee looked around and was quiet. She didn't question why I had silenced her; she just did as she was asked.

"I see them now," I said, spotting a couple of coyotes sneaking their way through the undergrowth. "It is okay, Rhymee. We can talk."

I looked over and noticed she had begun to perspire. She swallowed deeply as if suppressing fear.

"Good! What was it?" she asked, searching the dark sky.

"Coyotes…"

"Oh—"

"Rhymee, why do you look toward the sky for danger?"

"I…it was just a crazy notion," she said, acting like it was no big deal.

"It was not a crazy notion if it caused you to break a sweat."

"It's not that I was scared. I'm not a coward. I had an adrenaline rush. Obviously, you had a good reason for asking me to be quiet."

"Rhymee, please tell me. I know there was something else causing your stress." I knew what haunted her, but I wanted her to confide in me. I didn't want her knowing that I had seen her dream or that I knew the creatures were real.

She hesitated.

"You'll think I'm mad," she said.

"I have watched you grow up, and I know something or someone terrifies you. You are not mad."

"Well, you know how I can sense things sometimes?"

"Yes, and your senses are usually right on target."

"Okay, well something, not someone, wants to hurt me and my family, but I can't explain what it is. I feel it holds no real power, but it terrifies me. It's been gone for a long while, but I became naturally defensive when you asked me to be quiet. The real question is, why me, Thadacus? I've tried to tell myself it's just my imagination, but as I know when you come and go, I know when it lurks. It has a vile quality," she said, shivering.

I wanted to hold her. I started to offer my hand but stopped, remembering the magic flowing within me would shock her.

She reached for me as well, but she pulled back at the same time.

"I believe you, and I will not let anything hurt you."

"I know."

I could see Rhymee flush in the darkness. She didn't say anything.

I was quiet for a moment, trying to build up my nerve.

"Rhymee, I have a gift for you," I said, pulling the chain holding the miniature likeness of Thor's hammer from my pocket.

"What is it, Thad?" she eagerly asked.

"It is quite ancient," I said, handing her the trinket. "You cannot see it right now, but it is a necklace. Keep it hidden under your shirt while you are at school because I am not supposed to have it. I took it from an excavation site."

"Thank you. I'll always wear it," she said, connecting the chain around her neck. "I suppose I should get back inside."

"Good idea. It is late," I said.

She smiled, her face turning even a deeper shade of red.

We slowed our pace, trying to prolong our time together. I quietly thought of the future. I could not imagine deserting her as Egan had Savora. Death was once my greatest fear, but the thought of losing Rhymee had taken its place.

SOONER THAN EXPECTED

1988

That first meeting at the pond was followed by many more. Rhymee and I met as often as we could.

She had decided to go to a local university so she could remain near her family. I would have followed her anywhere, but she knew her parents were getting older, and she wanted to help them with any work that needed to be done around the farm.

It was Thanksgiving break, and Rhymee was looking forward to a restful weekend. She had pushed herself hard during finals and passed all her classes. She looked forward to late-night talks and walks with me without worrying about what time she had to start the next day.

"Rhymee, wake up! Mom is taking us shopping, remember? It's Black Friday. We're leaving in thirty minutes!" shouted Rhegan, pulling the covers off her sister.

Rhymee sluggishly slid her feet into her slippers. "I just wanted to sleep in for a change," she complained.

"Girls, are you ready?" hollered Bhren from the living room. "We are going to have to get to the mall early for the good deals!"

"Coming, Mom!" Rhymee's two sisters yelled, running down the stairs.

"Where's Rhymee?" asked Bhren.

"Here it comes. I'm getting told on," said Rhymee.

"She's not ready!" said Rhondel, sounding discouraged. "Do we have to wait on her?"

"I tried to wake her up!" Rhegan pointed out.

Rhymee opened the door to her room. "Mom, give me five minutes!" she shouted, tugging on her jeans.

"Fine! We will be waiting in the car," said Bhren, shooing her other two out the door.

On a normal day, I would not follow Rhymee to school or to town. I sensed she was run down. I was concerned, so I followed her that day.

There were so many people in the mall that no one noticed I wore sunglasses inside. I looked like a shopper, sporting a black leather jacket I purchased at a neighboring store a few minutes before. I pretended I was looking at items to purchase as I followed at a distance from store to store. Rhymee spotted me at one point and subtly waved so that her mom and sisters would not see. She lagged behind them. Every few minutes someone would cut her off to either grab something from a shelf or to get ahead in line during checkout.

"Rhymee, get up here! What are you doing way back there?" Bhren asked while they were checking out at Newman's.

Rhymee was standing behind ten other people waiting to have their items rung up.

"Sorry, Mom. They just walked in front of me."

"Why didn't you say something?" asked Bhren loudly, giving the line dirty looks. The people who had so rudely cut acted like they hadn't heard a thing. One guy just whistled and looked the other direction.

"I don't know," whined Rhymee.

"Well, come on. We are going to stop for lunch after this," said Bhren, thinking lunch would reenergize her daughter.

"Yeah! We're hungry! Can we eat at the Kicken Chicken? I love their waffle fries with sweet and sour sauce," begged Rhondel.

"What do you want, Rhegan?" asked Bhren.

"I want to eat at the Taco Meet!" said Rhegan.

"Oh come on, Rhegan. We just had that last week. Plus, you can get a kids meal at Kicken Chicken. They have those miniature stuffed animals this week."

"Rhondel, I am ten and a half. I am too big for that!" argued Rhegan.

"Rhymee, you are the decider. Out of the two, where do you want to go?" asked Bhren.

Rhondel and Rhegan both had pleading looks upon their faces.

"I do not care. I'm not really hungry," said Rhymee. Neither place appealed to her.

"Well, Rhondel has a good point. We did eat at Taco Meet last week. I will be the tiebreaker. Let's go to Kicken Chicken," decided Bhren, already exhausted.

It was just as packed at the restaurant as anywhere else in town.

Rhondel carried an air of victory as she placed her order, and once Rhegan smelled the aroma of spicy, fried chicken, she was also happy.

I casually took an empty cup sitting near the trashcan. The receptacle was so full it was brimming over with foam cups and plastic forks. I stood next to the bathroom door, acting like I was waiting on someone and pretending to drink. Whispering through the air, I told Bhren to take Rhymee home. I could feel her loss of appetite and sore body.

"Rhymee, what do you want? You're next," directed Bhren.

"I'm not hungry. How many more stores do we have to visit?"

"We're done. After we eat, we are heading home. You need to eat something. You haven't eaten all day. It will make you feel better!"

Good, she heard me, I thought.

"Fine, I will take some fries and ice water," said Rhymee, giving in to her mom. She knew it wasn't worth arguing over food, especially in this line.

"Anything else, ma'am?" the cashier asked with an annoyed look.

"I will also take a number five with lemonade, an extra order of fries, and an ice water," quickly responded Bhren.

Within seconds, the cashier produced a receipt.

"You're number twenty-six. Please take a seat. We will call your number when your order is ready."

"Like we didn't know to do that," said Rhymee, daring the cashier to retaliate.

"Rhymee!" exclaimed Bhren, pushing her daughter's back in the direction of the booth were Rhondel and Rhegan were patiently sitting.

"Well, I'm tired of people being rude today!" Rhymee defended, still staring at the girl.

Rhymee only ate a couple fries while her sisters gorged on their food.

"Rhymee, what is wrong with you? You haven't acted like yourself all day. Do you feel all right?" asked Bhren, placing her hand on Rhymee's forehead.

"I'm sorry, Mom. I don't mean to be a party pooper. I just feel tired. It's been a stressful semester. I'll be okay after I get some rest," said Rhymee, reassuring her mother.

A cold front moved in along with a rainstorm, and before nightfall, it began to sleet. I found the weather quite exhilarating, but I didn't want Rhymee venturing out to meet me.

It was easier to talk to her without interruptions from her family because she had moved out of the room she had once shared with her sisters. Her parents had converted the garage into a spare room. They had added new insulation, sheet rock, a window, and carpet. Then they built a separate two-car garage, which was no longer attached to the house. The new room was Rhymee's high school graduation gift.

I could hear her parents. They were still awake, but they were finally turning in. From ten to midnight, they worked hard putting up the Christmas tree and all the decorations. They had put it up a little early, wanting to surprise the girls.

"I'm glad you guys got your shopping done today. The roads aren't going to be in good shape tomorrow. The rain is starting to freeze," Richard said to Bhren, taking a last look out the door before locking it.

"It sounds like we are in the middle of a skillet full of sizzling bacon." Bhren laughed, leaning over her husband's shoulder to take a peek.

"Well, at least sizzling bacon doesn't freeze your butt off. It's more like cold baloney out there," said Richard, shivering as he shut the door.

I chuckled from beneath Rhymee's window.

"I'm happy to be iced in after the day I had," said Bhren, sounding tired. "Besides, Rhymee needs to unwind tomorrow."

I waited another hour before tapping on Rhymee's window. She was in bed but still awake.

"I'm sorry, Thad. Hold on," she said, slowly rising and making her way over to the window to unlock it.

My good mood was soured upon seeing her. She had no color, save the dark circles under her eyes.

"Rhymee, what is wrong? You do not look well," I asked, gently closing the window behind me.

"I must have the flu. Strange, huh? As far as I know, there haven't been that many cases. I haven't caught it in four years. Apparently I contract a weird strain when no one else does. Oddly, I'm not running a fever yet. You're lucky you don't have to feel this way anymore, Thad," she said, crawling back under the covers.

"You should go to the doctor tomorrow," I said.

"You know I'm tougher than that. The doctor would just charge me a hundred or more dollars for a ten-minute visit to tell me what I already know and then prescribe me some kind of over-the-counter hot drink mix to flush out my virus."

I knew she was right. The medical field had evolved from a fumbling butcher to a stitch-em-and-ditch-em assembly line since my time, so I didn't argue.

"Will it upset you if I'm poor company?"

"It will upset me if you do not rest," I said firmly. "No more talking! Close your eyes."

"Please stay. I always sleep better when you're here," she requested in a faded voice.

"I'll wake you a little before sunrise," I said, sitting down on the floor in the corner of the room.

Rhymee smiled weakly before rolling over and shutting her eyes.

Rhymee didn't return to school the following Monday. Her bones had begun to ache. By Tuesday, she reluctantly gave in and went to the doctor. I asked her if I could follow and listen from the waiting room, and she quickly agreed.

Dr. Ikie went through a list of questions.

"So tell me your symptoms, Miss Stewart," he asked.

111

Bhren responded for Rhymee. "Well, her bones ache, and she has no energy. She can barely get out of bed."

"I asked Rhymee!" the doctor pointed out. "I want to hear it from her."

Rhymee didn't like anyone speaking that way to her mom.

"No, she can speak for me just fine. I don't feel like answering your questions, and my mom is covering your bill."

"I'll be back in a minute," he said, leaving the room quickly.

Soon a young nurse came in and handed Bhren a prescription.

"Dr. Ikie has another patient to tend, but he has instructed me to tell you to get lots of rest. You have the flu. Keep bundled, stay indoors, and drink a lot of liquids. If your symptoms don't improve, we will see you back in a week," said the nurse in a sickeningly sweet tone.

I could imagine Rhymee giving the nurse a searing look.

"Do you have any other questions?" asked the nurse.

"No, but thanks," responded Bhren politely.

"What a waste of money," said Rhymee right before the nurse left the room.

"She heard you, Rhymee!" said Bhren, embarrassed.

"Good! Maybe she will pass how I feel along to the doctor."

"Oh, I'm sure the doctor knows how you feel."

"Mom, let's just go home before I lash out at someone else. I'm sorry I'm so cranky."

"It's okay. It's to be expected."

Over the next week, Rhymee's symptoms worsened. She could no longer hold down her food.

"Rhymee, I brought you some soup," offered Bhren, setting the bowl down on the nightstand. "Try and eat. Here in a while, your dad and I are taking you back to the doctor."

"I can't eat that, Mom. I will just throw it back up," responded Rhymee, becoming nauseated by the aroma. "I don't want to go back to Dr. Ikie. I can't stand him," she said feebly.

"We are taking you to someone else. I feel the same way," said Bhren. "Let me help you slide on your shoes."

"Mom, I don't want to go anywhere. I just want to be left alone," argued Rhymee in the nicest voice she could muster.

"Too bad. You might be eighteen now, but your dad and I still know what's best for you! I am not going to stand by while you rot away in this bed!"

"Fine!" said Rhymee, defeated, knowing better than to cross her mom when she took that tone.

"Here comes your dad."

Richard and Bhren were solemn and frustrated Christmas Eve. The day before, Dr. Blancard had told them he suspected cancer, but he would not know for certain until after the holidays because it took time to get the lab results back on all the blood work and tissue samples he had taken. Her parents didn't like waiting.

Rhymee had been in and out of the hospital, but she had been sent home for Christmas. She managed to hold some food down now and then, but she had lost a lot of weight. Every bone in her body was clearly defined.

Her parents had not told her anything, but she suspected bad news.

It was hard to hunt; I did not want to leave her. Even during nights at the hospital, I kept watch over her from the wide ledge outside her room's window. It pained me to return to the farm each day, but I found a little comfort knowing that either Richard or Bhren was constantly with her.

Her parents were upstairs wrapping last-minute gifts and talking privately. I could hear them clearly.

"Richard, if it is cancer, how are we going to tell her?" sobbed Bhren.

"It will be okay. Rhymee is a strong girl. We have to remain optimistic and keep our faith. She may have something else. We don't know anything yet. Don't let what Dr. Blancard said scare you. He could be way off," said Richard. He was terrified for his daughter.

"You're right! I need to stop crying so the girls won't suspect anything," said Bhren, wiping her face with her sleeve.

I had not cried in over two centuries, but no matter how hard I tried, I couldn't contain my emotions that night.

It was a rare occurrence for a vampire to shed tears and never a good idea. It was a great loss of energy, which meant I wouldn't be able to go much longer without feeding. My tears were no longer wet drops of saline like a human's. Instead, small balls of bluish-white energy would emerge from my tear ducts and float through the air.

I didn't think at that late hour anyone would take notice of my sadness, but I was wrong. Rhegan had grown thirsty and got up to get herself a drink. She noticed the glow from the window. Once she looked outside, she didn't hesitate to rush to her parents' room.

"Mom! Dad! Are you guys awake?" she asked, tapping at their door. She didn't care if she woke them.

"Yes, Rhegan, hold on," said Richard. I could hear them quickly shoving all the wrapped boxes, paper, and scissors back into the closet before opening the door.

I leaped to the roof.

"Come and look outside," insisted Rhegan, leading the way. Richard and Bhren followed.

"What are those?" asked Rhegan, pointing to the mysterious orbs floating outside.

They all three stood on the front porch speechless.

Listening to them took my mind off Rhymee for a second, so I was able to stop crying momentarily.

"Well, I have never personally seen anything like this, but my friend Bob Sheemaker once told me a story where he described something similar," said Richard.

"Go on," said Bhren, cautiously watching the orbs.

"Halloween night, a long time ago, he and one of his buddies tried to stay the night in an old graveyard where most everyone had died of small pox because he had heard reports of strange lights, which supposedly appeared on occasion out of the blue in that area. The local neighbors near the cemetery began to call them spook lights. I guess seeing is believing. He and his friend Joe hightailed it out of there after witnessing the phenomenon for themselves. They were scared to death. He has told everyone that story for years now, but I never took him seriously until now," said Richard.

"Do you think they are dangerous?" asked Bhren, holding Rhegan's hand tightly, in case she needed to dart back inside with her.

Richard hesitated for a moment before answering.

"No, I also watched a documentary on lightning balls, but I don't think that is what this is because it hasn't been storming."

"I wish Rhymee could see this. She could probably give us a better explanation, but it's not worth waking her," said Bhren cheerlessly.

"You are right," said Richard.

"Rhegan, let's go back inside," suggested Bhren.

"You go ahead. I will be in shortly," said Richard, wanting to watch a little longer.

I lay flat against the rough shingles. Bhren had been right. Rhymee would have known exactly what the balls of light were because in one of our numerous conversations, I had told her what happened when vampires wept. I was glad she was sleeping at that moment; I didn't want her to know I had been crying.

After long debate, I concluded I had caused her illness. It had come much sooner than expected. The night I bit her I felt confident in my decision because I wanted her to live life to its fullest, but now I deeply regretted biting her. Her fears were real, not a figment of her imagination as I once assumed. The thought of losing her made my heart twist into knots. I had to do something, but what? Could the magic be reversed? Egan would have known what to do. Curse him for leaving me.

CONFESSION

After my tears floated away, I decided to hunt. I couldn't help Rhymee in a weakened state. The magic flowing through me was drained even before I had begun to cry. There wasn't enough left to transfer from my fangs to her body. A second bite would buy her some time, but not long; it might give her the false hope she was cured for another six months or so.

I crept in her room, sat in the corner, and watched her for a long while. One of my tears had followed me in and now hovered near the ceiling, radiating like a disco light.

I decided to place her in a deep sleep until I returned. I slowly made my way to her bedside, but before I could breathe, she suddenly woke.

"Thad?" she faintly asked.

"I am here, angel," I answered gently.

"I knew it was you. My room smells like you."

"Rhymee, I need to hunt, but I will return soon."

"Thad, I want to die alone. Take me from here. I don't want my parents or sisters to see, and the time is coming."

"Rhymee, listen to me! I am going to help you, but you must hold on! Do you understand?"

"You know I will fight death until I've no strength left, but unfortunately my strength is fading. When I'm conscious and the pain subsides, I feel as if I'm just a piece of furniture in the room. I can see people and objects, but I no longer understand their actions or purpose. I'm numb."

"Rhymee, you need to hang on just a little longer."

"What can you do, Thad? I can't become a vampire. There are currently five hundred, and I would never ask one of them to die for me. I couldn't live with that guilt, and besides, what would my parents say? I know they would never understand."

I took a deep breath, again fighting to hold back my tears.

"I don't understand why I'm so sick, but it is inevitable that I die. It doesn't scare me to die. I only regret that I wasn't allowed to grow old. I don't want to miss out on anything. I've done so little. I wonder what my destiny really was. It obviously was not fulfilled."

"Rhymee, trust me. I can help you!"

"Most of all, I don't want to leave you, Thadacus. I love you," she earnestly stated. Tears were streaming down her face.

"I love you too, Rhymee. I wish I could take your place and suffer for you. Promise me you will hang on until I can return from my hunt in a few days. Prove to me you are a fighter."

"I pro…"

She scared me when she stopped mid sentence and stared at the ceiling. "What is it?"

"What is that?" she asked with great interest, trying to lift her head up farther.

"What? Oh, I was, uh…"

"You were, oh…"

She knew what had caused the orb after giving it some thought but didn't say it out loud. She didn't want to embarrass me, not that it would have.

"May I keep it?"

"I suppose. It will not last much longer. It will be gone by morning."

"Thad, I promise I will be here when you return. Take your time hunting."

I leaned over her and exhaled deeply into her nostrils. She would not wake until I called for her, but her parents would think she was resting soundly.

"Sip and swallow," I requested, feeding her water by the teaspoonful over the next hour.

I knew she held a better chance of holding it down in small dosages. Hopefully, it would help sustain her a little longer.

I stopped in Prairie Grove and picked up a copy of *The Arkansas Reporter* and searched the headlines for criminal activity. The front page contained nothing but pictures of a semi that had flipped over and wounded the driver. He was in critical condition and wasn't expected to live. I was tempted to feed upon him. It was the easiest choice. I could sneak in, feed, and return to Rhymee within a few hours. I debated for a moment, but once I played the scene through my mind, I knew I could not carry through with it. Rhymee would not want to cause that man's death either. She would never forgive me, and I knew I would never forgive myself.

I kept searching but found nothing else of interest. I would have to hunt the old-fashioned way by seeking out the most secluded, dangerous spots and then waiting for a vile human to perform a vile act. Rest stops, dark alleys, parks, and abandoned buildings were places where I usually found the most action.

Unfortunately, Prairie Grove and the surrounding cities were usually pretty safe. It meant I would have to travel farther, and since I lacked energy, I would move at a much slower pace.

After searching with no luck at all, I decided to try one of my old tricks I used at the many pubs in Europe and lure the wicked to me. It took a grueling two days before one took the bait. I gave my description, where I would be waiting, and spread the word that I was in the market for guns without serial numbers. A couple hours later, a man cautiously walked up the sidewalk, smoking a cigarette. He inhaled, causing his cigarette to burn bright orange at the tip.

"Who are you?" he asked. "I haven't seen you around here before."

"I'm from out of town. I don't want anyone to know what I need," I answered coolly.

"What do you need?" he asked.

I searched through the darkness. There were a few people in the area. I could smell alcohol on one as he staggered incoherently on the opposite sidewalk. The other, I assumed, was this man's partner. She sat in a vehicle three blocks away, watching us at a distance.

"Firearms."

"Have you got cash? They are not cheap."

I pulled a roll of cash from my pocket. "Take a look."

He leaned forward, and when he did, I bit the front of his throat while pinning his hands. He couldn't scream. I fed quickly and to my fullest. When I let him fall to the ground, I thought the girl watching would scream. Instead, she fumbled with her keys until she finally stuck the correct one in the ignition, waited nervously as the engine turned over a few times before it started, and hit the gas so hard that she peeled out of her parking spot. I guess she didn't want to stick around the crime scene.

I raced back to Rhymee.

It was daybreak when I arrived at the farm. Rhymee was alive, barely, and constantly surrounded by hospice and family. I would have to wait till dark and find a way to lure the nurse away from her. In the meantime, I sought solitude and darkness in the well.

It had been a quiet day, but it was a windy, noisy evening. Dead leaves rustled in the trees, wind chimes clanged, and I could hear a pack of coyotes howling. Was it some kind of mysterious sign?

"Rhymee, wake up. I have returned." Her bedroom window was cracked to allow a breeze to circulate through her room. She woke instantly.

I stood behind a tree, watching, trying to think of a plan, but Rhymee took care of the nurse.

"Please leave! I want to be alone!" she demanded in a laborious tone.

"It's not a good idea, dear!" said Nurse Walker assertively.

"Leave! Leave before I use the last bit of energy I have to run you out, and do not come back this night!"

"As you wish! I will let your parents know you want to be alone," said the nurse, sounding like a tattletale.

"Whatever!" responded Rhymee.

That's my girl, I thought.

"Thad, I know you have returned. The breeze carries your scent. Hurry! The window is cracked! I can't hold out much more!" she gasped.

There was no time to put her to sleep. Plus, I knew the nurse would return soon with Rhymee's parents. I rushed to her bed and knelt on the carpet.

"I'm glad you made it back. I wanted to look upon you one last time."

"Rhymee, do you trust me?" I quickly asked.

"Yes."

"This will hurt, but you must remain silent."

Her eyes widened in shock; then she reluctantly nodded. "What do I have to lose?" she said.

I reached under her back and lifted her to me. Then with my free hand I sealed her mouth while biting deeply into her neck, avoiding her jugular vein. Even though she had promised to remain quiet, she struggled, snorting heavily with bubbled cheeks. She wanted to scream from the pain.

I did not drink her blood. However, during the transfer, it was necessary to swallow some. Those were the longest seconds as I suffered from that rancid taste. Consuming even the smallest amount had made my stomach churn. Her blood burned my throat like bleach and tasted like a mixture of fish oil and raw yeast.

The deed was done, so I wasted no time in leaving the room. I was ill.

Feeling queasy, I slouched down behind a tree.

Within moments, Rhymee had recovered enough to stand. "Thad!" she called, not understanding why I fled so quickly.

"Your parents are coming," I whispered. "You best get back in bed. They won't understand your miraculous recovery. We will talk later."

"Thank you," she said with quiet intensity.

"What, well I—" The nurse opened the door to find Rhymee on her feet. "Miss Stewart, what are you doing?" she asked, disbelieving her eyes.

Her parents soon followed.

"Rhymee!" stated Bhren in blissful shock.

"Mom! Dad! I feel better!" said Rhymee, quickly covering her neck with the thick collar of her robe.

Richard simply walked over, grabbed her, and lifted her off the floor, squeezing her as tightly as he could without cutting off her air supply.

"Great, honey, but you should probably get back in bed. We will call Dr. Blancard in the morning," said Bhren, still having doubts about her daughter's health.

Nurse Walker walked over to take Rhymee's temperature and check vitals.

"Don't touch me!" warned Rhymee, not caring if her dad and mom would get upset or not.

"Well, I…I have never dealt with someone more difficult!" said the nurse, directing her comment to Rhymee's parents in hopes they would scold her.

"Rhymee, you should let Nurse Walker check you," requested Richard.

"Dad, she enjoys sticking me with needles! When I was thirsty, she denied me water in hopes I would die faster! I was unconscious but still aware! She should be punished!"

Richard stared at the nurse, crinkling his brow. After a moment, he knew his daughter spoke the truth.

"I'm leaving!" Nurse Walker said. "I can't stay another second in this house with you crazy people."

I wanted to rip her hospice throat out, but I was too sick to move. I told myself, *Another time perhaps.*

Rhymee's blood had become more noxious with age. There was a rancid aftertaste I could not shake.

I crawled, inching my way to the well. Not really caring how I landed, I freefell to the bottom and then leaned my cheek on the cold, wet, moss-covered stones. I gathered the muddy pooled water with my palms and splashed my face, and then I used it like mouthwash to rinse her blood from between my teeth. It had no effect. Her bad blood was consuming me.

I pulled slimy moss off the surrounding rocks and chewed it like gum and spit it out. That helped a little but not nearly enough. I ebbed slowly into a crouched position and stayed that way for over a week.

"Thad, why haven't you come to me?" asked Rhymee. "What have I done? I don't understand. I know you're hiding in the well."

I couldn't answer. In my mind, I had to remember I loathed her blood, not her. Had the vile substance poisoned my heart?

Several days later, I heard her crying for me, but I couldn't bring myself to move. However, I did give her a short response.

"Rhymee, give me some time," I answered, sounding severe but not intending to.

She didn't say another word and did as I requested, which helped. She was so different than any other woman I had known in so many ways. Not nagging was one of her superior qualities.

Maybe I was following the same path as Illisa, becoming less interested in Rhymee with each bite. I did not want to leave Rhymee, but the smell of her reminded me of her revolting blood.

Two weeks had passed when I heard her bedroom window slam shut. The sound aroused me from my meditation. I listened for a moment. I heard nothing else, so I dismissed it as inconsequential.

Moments later I heard steel raking. A blade was being pulled from a sheath. I leapt from the well.

Rhymee darted up the stairs to her sister's room, holding a knife. When she reached the door, she stopped and slowed her breathing. Slowly twisting the old white metal doorknob in hopes in wouldn't creak, she cautiously entered their room. She walked over to the window and silently stood there. At first, her heart pounded, but she slowly managed to take control of its pace.

She was guarding them.

I circled the yard a few times and stopped below the window.

"Rhymee, what is it?" I asked.

She looked right at me, acknowledged my presence, but did not answer.

"Are they back?"

She glanced at me sourly. I patiently stared back, knowing she was hurt and angry because I had ignored her for so long.

"I can handle this, Thadacus!" she finally whispered. Then she looked away, holding her knife firmly.

"What can I do to help?" I asked.

"You can't!" she said coldly.

At that moment, I remembered that I loved Rhymee. What had happened? I did not understand, and neither did she. I could feel her emotions. She was trying to show me her strength. She had hardened herself and prepared for the worst imaginable outcome: my leaving. Even though she would be heartbroken, she would never admit to it. Rhymee would never allow herself to show weakness. She was resolved. There would be no pleading, crying, bribing, or spouting hurtful words. Silence would be her farewell note.

How could I have been so poisoned? I was tortured knowing I had hurt her and that she no longer trusted me.

"Rhymee, please come outside! We need to talk. I was ill, but I am better!"

She just stared at me. She wasn't ready to destroy her stone wall. "Now is not a good time," she said, watching the sky.

"Then when?" I asked, sounding desperate.

"If you still wish to talk, then I will meet you tomorrow night."

I knew she needed some time to soften her anger.

Rhymee was not one to so easily forget a wrong. She would often hold her anger, protect it, and store it for a later, more useful date. Things that irritated her usually required much thought, and once her irritation reached a fury, there was no calming it. She would not harvest her rage into a fit or tantrum but rather convert it to memory, and then she would wait a lifetime to recall it when she needed it the most. She held a strong sense of right and wrong and thrived when given the opportunity to teach a lesson. Once the lesson had been taught, only then would her stagnant anger be laid to rest.

Her fury was making me sick. It was as if I had healed from one illness only to contract another one. I had to talk to her and explain that I did not intentionally abandon her, but I also knew not to press her. I needed to give her a little time to think.

"Get some sleep, Rhymee. I will not let anything hurt you or your sisters," I suggested, perceiving she no longer believed it.

When she slowly put the knife back in its sheath and sighed, I knew her wall had cracked.

It was agony waiting for the next evening, not only because I had come out of my stupor and now missed her, but also I dreaded the conversation I knew we must have.

During the early morning when most humans slept, Rhymee quietly cracked her window, knowing only I would hear and accept her invitation.

"Rhymee, may I come in?" I asked out of courtesy.

"Please do."

I entered to find her sitting in her chair, bundled up in thick blankets.

"I'm sorry for my rude behavior. There's no excuse," she apologized.

"You have every right to be angry, Rhymee. I am the one who is sorry. I was very sick," I explained.

"From what? I thought you were invincible."

"I do not know, but I was out of my mind," I explained.

I wasn't able to tell her she had been the cause and over the past few weeks I had loathed the scent of her.

"Was it from biting me?" she asked somberly. "You became ill right afterward."

"Absolutely not!" I didn't hesitate to lie.

By her expression, I knew she didn't fully believe me. "Thad, since you bit me, I can recall early memories and forgotten dreams. Have you bit me before?" she asked, seeming to already know the answer.

I took a deep breath and sat down on my usual spot in the corner, preparing for my confession.

"I have," I carefully responded.

"Why?" she asked unpretentiously. "I am not angry. I just—"

"Rhymee, do you remember what you felt like when you would break out into hives, or when you would lie awake at night, pretending you were encased in an impenetrable wall of steel just so you could sleep? Terror had taken hold of you and was controlling you. I thought the magic held within my bite could bring you out of that."

"But what I am frightened of is real!"

"I know that now. I made a horrible mistake. I should not have interfered," I said.

"I am glad you did, Thadacus. Otherwise, I would probably have gone crazy knowing something was out there haunting me but not being able to understand or see its true form. I don't understand why you can't see the reddish-purple haze looming in the sky that even sometimes appears during the day."

"Do not say you are glad yet. I have not told you everything," I said gravely.

She seemed puzzled but then appeared enlightened.

I struggled for the right words.

"Thad, this power you've given me has made me a little clairvoyant. I know what you have caused," she said.

"What?" I asked, doubting her insight.

"I'm dying, right?"

I took a deep breath, trying to contain my emotions. "It's not supposed to happen like this. I don't understand why you are sick so soon. For centuries, vampires have bitten humans to help them overcome mental or physical disabilities. We know that in old age our magic will begin to work against the human body because its force is too powerful to be permanently contained," I admitted. My eyes glazed over with tears. "There must be something wrong with me to cause the reaction this soon."

"Thad, I'm not mad at you. I understand why you did it," she said.

"Rhymee, the second bite has only bought you a short amount of time. In the end, it will accelerate the process. I must bite you a third time to completely change you."

"I don't understand! If the magic is already killing me, how is a third dose of it going to help?" she asked.

"The magic will destroy the weaknesses within your flesh. It converts your entire physical makeup. Even though you will appear somewhat the same, you will no longer be as you are. You shall still die, in a sense, but the most powerful part of you will remain, your soul."

"Let me guess! It will hurt."

I cringed as I nodded in agreement. "The pain does not last long."

"That's a comfort," she said cynically.

"It may not happen anyway. I must seek permission from the vampire council, the Ragnvaldr. Our leaders must approve of it, and you already know our number is currently met."

"The what? What is your council called?" she asked.

I laughed at her curiosity because I had asked Egan the same question years ago.

"Long ago, Dario, one of the first vampires to inhabit earth, had watched the ways and conquests of the ancient Norse Jarlabanke Clan, and he felt great respect for two warriors of the clan, Invar and his son, Ragnvald Ingvarrson. After they were killed in battle, Dario wanted to honor his fallen human friends, and he eventually found a way. Centuries later, he decided to name his vampire council the Ragnvaldr."

Rhymee thought about my story for a moment. "That's an interesting history, but I won't let someone else die for me."

"I could never ask that, but I will request that the rule be bent. I will ask that they make room for one more."

"The thing or things lingering outside are listening to us right now. I'll admit I don't want you to leave me to face them alone."

"I do not understand why I cannot see them or why they haunt you, but I do know they hold no physical power, or they would have killed you and your family long ago," I explained.

"Maybe they haven't hurt me or my family because you were here!"

"But I have left before, so that could not be the case."

"What if I don't want to become a vampire?" she asked combatively.

"You, who would battle death to the end, wish to die instead?" I asked, astounded by her sudden question.

"I feel like there's a lot to consider, and there's no time."

I put my head down. I knew what troubled her. I didn't have a choice when I was turned. If I had been given the choice, what path would I have taken? "What weighs on your mind?"

"I think about living forever, and I wonder if I could so easily watch my family pass away of old age. I don't know if I want to outlive them."

"Do you want them to have to watch you die? Which will be harder? Do you want your mom, dad, sisters, and I have to watch you be put in the ground?"

I wanted to tell her that hunting would be the hardest thing, but I could not make myself bring up the subject. I did not want her to choose death.

She sighed.

Through all her understanding, I still felt guilty for the pain and suffering I had inflicted upon her.

"I know you need to think about the decision you must make."

She slightly nodded but did not give an answer, so I changed the subject. "I am sorry the bite hurt. I tried to do it quickly to cause you the least amount of pain."

"I'd prepared myself for the pain of your bite, but I'd forgotten about the shock that comes from your touch."

My head sank between my knees in regret.

Unexpectedly, she walked over and grabbed my hands, pulling me up from the floor. "Don't stress out, and don't worry about me while you're away. I can take care of myself," she said.

I jerked my hands free. Did I hear her correctly? Was she going to agree to be turned? "Rhymee, why would you touch me, knowing what happens?"

"You should know the answer to that by now," she said, seeming a little disappointed in my reaction.

"It's not that I… It's just—"

Taking a deep breath, she lunged and jumped, locking her legs around my hips. Throwing her arms around my neck, she forcefully kissed me and then allowed herself to fall.

Her skin and lips were splotched with red streaks.

"Do you know how I feel, that I crave you and your stinging touch?" she stated with devastating conviction.

I didn't say a word. Instead, I pulled her up and deeply kissed her. I did not let go until I could taste the salt from her streaming tears.

"Thadacus! Go! Go and ask your Ragnvaldr! I don't want to leave you, and I don't want to die!"

Early the next night, I kissed Rhymee good-bye and left feeling weighted with dread. I pushed myself forward apprehensively, fearing I would not make it back quickly enough to save her. Time was of little consequence to Frost and his council. I had heard rumors they never usually reached a quick decision, and what if they said no? Deep down, I knew I would break the rules regardless. I sought permission because I didn't want another fight on my hands, and I didn't want to endanger Rhymee any more than I already had.

KARNAK NHU

Henry Frost, our current Ragnvaldr leader, chose to keep all private records and hold the council's meetings in an ancient, abandoned coal mine, which over time the vampires had renovated. The mine was located in Alberta, Canada.

The entrance to the old quarry was small and heavily guarded. Vampires were the only ones who could visit unannounced.

Mountainous forest surrounded the mine. Frost owned all of it and had for centuries.

I had never visited, but I had an idea of where to go based on the information Egan had shared with me. He had described a tiny cabin lacking fineries, yet cozy, positioned on the outskirts of the property. It had been built early in the twentieth century with a sod roof, dirt floors, and cedar logs chinked with a mixture of red clay, rocks, and dried grass.

I am close, I thought, beginning to smell the residue of unfamiliar vampires. Rhymee was troubled, so I was too. I knew she had received some kind of warning. I was tempted to turn around and go to her, but I knew she would surely die if I did not continue my quest.

Climbing upward on a wooded hill, I noticed the trail began to widen. I slowed down, becoming more cautious. I was not in a sociable mood and hoped I could avoid other vampires until I was ready to speak.

Upon reaching the top, I was shocked to see a new log home with glass windowpanes, plumbing, and a large covered porch nestled in a grass-covered valley; it was not what I had pictured.

With no barriers to hold it back or slow it down, the wind was a battering force along the ridge. I stood my ground against its might like a deeply rooted tree, taking in all the scents it carried.

After all these years, it cannot be. My nose betrays me, I thought. I took in another deep breath. A faint mixture of rose oil and dirt from land that I had plowed long ago as a human tainted the air and confirmed my hunch that someone I knew was inside the cabin.

Why is she here? I thought, heading down the slope. Upon reaching the front yard, I stopped and patiently waited. I assumed it would not be long before my scent was detected. Besides, I was leery of stepping on the porch of a strange place. I recalled warnings from my childhood never to trust strangers or unfamiliar territory. Even though I was virtually indestructible, I was still a young vampire, not holding the wisdom of my predecessors or their lack of caution and fear.

A curtain was slightly pulled to the side; then a moment later the cabin door slowly creaked open.

A tall, slender vampire with thick lips, high cheekbones, and curly hair the color of melted chocolate warily stepped out on the porch. For a second, she looked torn between disappointment and joy.

"Come in, Thad," Illissa motioned, giving me an approving look with her coffee-colored eyes.

Hmm, guess she decided to go the hospitable route, I thought. I replied by frowning and guardedly stepped through the door.

"Glad to see you too," she said, smiling casually. "Make yourself comfortable. You arrived just in time. Another thirty minutes and you would have been blind."

"I arrived exactly when I meant to."

It was easy for me to be impolite. Obviously I was resentful for her having left without a good-bye or an explanation and for shunning me away for years.

I sat down in a small, blue, well-cushioned recliner, really too soft for my taste.

"Why are you here?" she asked, taking a seat across from me and acting like it was no big deal I had suddenly shown up without an invitation.

"I could ask the same of you," I replied sharply.

"I am staying here for a while."

"Why?" I asked.

"It is none of your concern, Thadacus Goodridge. Technically you are in my territory, so I should be the one to ask that question. Tell me. Why are you here?"

"I need to meet with the Ragnvaldr," I said. I compared her to Rhymee unintentionally. Not only would I never find another woman to match Rhymee's beauty and kindness, but no other personality on earth would fit mine so well. *Everything truly happens for a reason*, I thought, thinking of how things had turned out.

"Why?" she asked curiously.

"I seek their knowledge," I said, withholding my motives. She looked at me questioningly, so I grew impatient and could not bite my tongue. "Look, I know it's hard for you to stay in the same room as me, but can you endure my presence long enough to help me? I need to know how I can request a meeting."

"I'll help you, Thadacus, but you don't understand. That is my fault. I apologize for avoiding you for as long as I have. It is not hard for me to be near you, and I care for you just as much now as I did many years ago," she explained and then paused, waiting for my response.

I was not willing to pardon her behavior. "Then why have you not spoken to me since the day you changed me? When I tried to seek you out, you ran from me! Mysteriously, after I was turned, Egan was the vampire in my new existence!"

"I had to flee," she said plainly.

"For what reason?"

"Well, I suppose it will not hurt you to know since many years have passed. I turned you without permission. You see, there was no time. Do you remember the day you woke as a vampire? It was midday, you know. Do you not find it odd? Have you known any other vampire to wake from a turning at midday?" Her know-it-all personality was shining through. I did not like that about her.

"Well, let me see… Oh, yeah, I have not been to any turnings, so I suppose I wouldn't know, Illissa," I answered sarcastically.

She lifted an eyebrow, indicating she didn't like my comment. "Try," she pressed.

I sat there for a while, quietly reflecting on the past. Illissa waited patiently for my response.

"I remember the day clearly."

"Do you remember anything before that?" she asked.

"I can remember chasing you through my snow-covered field. The snow was knee deep, and I couldn't keep up with you. You were so fast. Then I remembered seeing your face through blurred vision. That is all," I said, disappointed I could not recall more.

"Back then, or even now, it is not common for a young man to collapse from heart failure, but you did in the field that very night. One second you were laughing and running after me, and then the next you were falling to the ground. Until that moment, I had not intended on biting you, Thadacus. You were perfect in every way. You did not need a vampire's magic, or so I thought. Upon finding you there, collapsed and lifeless, I was immediately compelled to help you. I bit you a hundred times that night. I bit you so many times your puncture wounds began to glow."

She stopped and put her head down.

"Why so many bites, Illissa?" I asked.

"Panic consumed me. I did something no other before me had done," she said.

At that moment, I didn't know if I wanted her to continue by the look she was giving me.

"What are you talking about?" I slowly asked.

"I knew you were already dead when I administered the bites, and the magic did not immediately take effect."

"How long did it take?" I asked, thinking it could not have been more than a few minutes.

"I waited five days then finally buried you."

My mouth fell open.

"Egan was my close friend long before he was yours," she said, sounding a little selfish, "so I sought his advice. He was livid and warned that I would be executed once the council found out about my treachery. At that point, I did not care about my fate. I still felt like I could somehow save you. I begged him to come back with me. His curiosity got the best of him, and he finally agreed. Your grave had remained undisturbed."

Even though my magical body would not allow it, I felt like I needed to be covered in goose bumps. "How long, Illissa? How long was I buried?" I asked, cringing at the thought of being buried alive.

"Not long… Egan wanted to examine your body, so he dug you up."

"You didn't help?" I crossly asked.

She sighed wearily then continued her story. "We found you in the same condition. You had not decayed in the least, and your puncture wounds had fully healed."

"How comforting," I snapped.

Illissa was quiet for a moment and seemed ashamed.

"Thadacus, you did not stir for eight and a half years. For months, Egan and I did everything we could to wake you, but you remained asleep."

"Eight and a half years?" I asked, stunned.

Illissa shrugged. "Yes."

Something deep down, something intimidating, a memory perhaps, at that moment was aroused, but I instinctively knew I was not ready to understand the notion, so I quickly suppressed it. I was dealing with enough. I would work on remembering what had happened to me long ago another time.

"I woke to find Egan instead of you. He gave me your letter—you know, the one explaining how you never wanted to see me again and not to come after you."

"Egan kept watch over you at my request," she defended. I went directly to the Ragnvaldr and explained what I had done, expecting the worst punishment—death."

"There are far worse things to endure other than death," I pointed out.

"I know, but at the time, I was not ready to die. I was terrified. To my disbelief, after hearing my case, Frost understood why I had done things the way I had. I was free to go. However, because I did not seek the Ragnvaldr's permission, I was not permitted to visit you in the instance you should wake. I wrote the letter to make it easier for you to let me go.

To be fully honest, I did not think you would ever wake. It disgusted me that my magic was trapped inside your corpse and I could not regain it. I felt I had wasted the gift of my bite during those eight and a half years of your slumber. You were kept away, hidden from the vampire community. Beyond me, only Egan and the council knew of your odd existence. When you came around, Egan sent word to me. By that point, it was easy to stay clear because my feelings slowly faded. However, I finally felt my magic had fulfilled its purpose and I had not given it to a fruitless end. I truly believe you are here because you have a destiny to fulfill as a vampire, and, upon much reflection, I am happy to have played a part in that."

"Then you are breaking the rules right now, are you not?"

"I suppose I am, but I doubt Frost will punish me," she responded, finding my comment amusing for some reason. "Do you harbor ill will toward me, Thadacus?"

"I feel nothing toward you, Illissa, whether it be hate or love. You're just a vampire who, in my eyes, cannot obey the rules set forth by the council," I answered bitterly. I was not for any reason going to give her the pleasure of knowing that I still cared for her.

"Well, now that we have gotten all that out of the way, the council has been meeting every evening. I am sure Frost and the others will grant you an audience. You can accompany me, if you wish. I have attended several meetings."

"Why are you here, Illissa?" I asked, deducing she had some peculiar reason.

"You shall find out soon enough. Now, I wish to meditate. I will admit seeing you has slightly upset me, and our conversation was tiring. I need to rest my mind so that I am clear headed for our meeting tonight. Please excuse me and make yourself at home," she said, exiting into the next room.

Gladly, I thought. She was right; the conversation had not been at all gratifying. I spent the rest of the day thinking of how I would approach Frost and trying to guess what type of vampire he was. Would I like him or despise him?

That evening we entered the portal of the coal mine. It was not at all what I had envisioned. I had heard the mine had been reconstructed like the cabin, but it was dark, musty, and smelled of death. About three-quarters of a mile down, shafts supported by the same wooden beams installed over a century ago darted out in several directions.

"Miners were killed down here, you know, during a cave-in. The fallen rock was so piled and compacted, the survivors could not retrieve the sealed off bodies. This place became their permanent tombs," explained Illissa, sounding like some sort of tour guide. "Can you guess which direction?"

I stopped for a moment and sniffed the air.

"That way," I said, pointing to one of the tunnels, located to the left.

"You are correct," she said, continuing her slow pace forward.

My curiosity had gotten the best of me, and I found myself straying in the direction of the dead.

"Thadacus, what are…"

Illissa turned to find I was no longer following her. I wondered if the miners' bones were still there.

"Thadacus! We are not allowed to disturb them! Frost's orders!" she said, running toward me.

"I am not stupid, Illissa. I gathered that by the looks of things."

"Well, we need to move. The council will not wait for our late arrival."

"Then lead the way, my dear," I said, exasperated.

We came to a thick oak door. Illissa opened it without hesitation as if it were a door inside her own house. Once we entered, I found the walls lined with shelves of books and journals coated in dust.

"This is where the storage begins," she said.

"The storage of what?"

She stopped and looked at me as if I was stupid.

"Obviously they are books, but of what?" I asked.

"They are full of anything vampires have found to be useful or important. Some are histories while others are records of past council meetings, the topics of interest, and the decisions our leaders have made and why they made them."

"May I?" I asked, wanting to pull one of the books down to read.

"Any vampire may read these, but we do not have time for that right now. Remember, you wanted to meet Frost. If we arrive late, they may take offense. You can read later."

"Are there records we are not permitted access to?"

"I know of only one book. Frost keeps it locked away most of the time, but I have seen him carry it around occasionally. It is definitely a history, and it is quite old. The council leader is the only one who inherits the privilege to read it."

"Hmmm," I responded.

Illissa continued to ramble on about the place, but I was not listening. If I had known these records were contained here, I would have visited long ago. We had entered into a vast labyrinth containing mountains of knowledge. I was dumfounded.

"Why do you suppose Egan didn't mention this?" I asked, angered because he had kept it secret.

"He is more interested in ancient artifacts or treasures of gold and silver. A lot of these records and histories were written during his time. My guess would be he lived through much of it, so the events are of no consequence to him."

I hadn't thought about the span of Egan's life. Her statement made sense.

"You are probably correct," I said, realizing I actually missed my old friend. "Don't you mean *were* of no consequence?"

"No, I meant are. Why don't you ask him yourself instead of speculating?"

"He is dead! He chose to go through the ceremony years ago," I contended.

"I beg to differ. I just had a lengthy conversation with him last night."

"What?" I asked in disbelief.

"Shhh, we're here!"

We arrived at another large wooden door same as the last, only this time it opened to a spacious room, which held several chairs and a long wooden table riddled with pockmarks and scuffs.

"Where is everyone? Are we too late?" I asked, confused by the fact we were the only ones there.

"We are a few minutes early. You know me. I am never late." She laughed.

"How early?"

"About half an hour," she responded.

"That is like you. I knew I should have grabbed a book!" I said, sitting beside her in one of the many chairs strewn around the room.

Soon vampires began to walk in and take seats. I had pictured them wearing long robes with hoods, but they were dressed in jeans or slacks along with button-up oxfords and tees.

"There's Henry Frost," Illissa whispered, pointing to the short, blonde man that had just entered the room and seated himself at the center of the long table. He was young, yet he looked wise. He didn't glance up even once. He was busy reading through a stack of papers that he had carried in with him.

"How do I request an audience?"

"That is not necessary. Your time to speak will come."

"How will I know?" I asked, studying Frost.

"Thad, I'm sure I don't need to introduce you to that vampire," interrupted Illissa, trying to gain my attention by thumping my knee.

In walked Egan, sporting a Hawaiian shirt and pair of green shorts.

"What the…" I said under my breath, staring him down.

He waved at me like it was no big deal he was still alive. He then took a seat next to Frost.

I jumped from my chair and stared at him coldly. He would not look at me. Instead, he began whispering to Frost and going through the papers with him.

Illissa tugged at my shirt. "Sit down. You will have your time to speak in a while."

I reluctantly took my seat.

Soon four more vampires arrived and sat at the large table. I didn't know any of them, but Illissa quickly filled me in.

"That is Mary Warren, Chris Cornwell, Floyd Harmon, and Haygen Hauden entering. They make up the rest of the council," she whispered.

By the time the meeting was called to order, fifty-two vampires from all over the world had taken seats to hear the Ragnvaldr speak.

Frost stood and addressed the audience. I continued to glare at Egan.

"Thank you for coming. This evening we must decide how to handle the rogues. I assume most of you are in attendance because I have sent for your help. Illissa, I want to thank you and your group for capturing the first one."

Illissa silently nodded with a smile.

"You are more than welcome to continue your stay at the cabin while you help us," offered Frost.

"What are you hunting? What rogues? What is going on?" I whispered, suddenly worried for her and turning away from Egan.

She placed her index finger over her lips. I felt like a schoolboy who had been caught passing notes.

"Listen, and you shall find out."

"Is anyone here for any other reason before we proceed?" asked Egan, gazing directly at me.

I looked around the room; it was quiet.

Illissa nudged me. "Go on," she whispered. "Now is the time to speak. You will not get another chance."

I quickly stood.

The council was suddenly staring at me intently, which was quite intimidating. I glanced at Egan, and he gave me an encouraging look.

"State your full name," ordered Mary Warren in a callous tone. She reminded me of a witch with her long, pointy nose, small beady eyes, and black hair tightly pulled away from her face.

I allowed myself a few seconds to remember Rhymee. The thought of her dying gave me the strength to boldly address the council in front of the large crowd.

"Thadacus Enman Goodridge."

Mary Warren quickly took notes.

"I have heard many things about you, Mr. Goodridge. It gives me pleasure to finally meet you," said Frost, gazing at me with curiosity. "What brings you here?"

"Two reasons."

"State the first," requested Frost.

"I seek permission to turn a human," I requested matter-of-factly.

"And the second?" asked Frost, seeming to give no thought to the first request.

I looked at the crowd for a moment. They would all think I was crazy. How could I describe what Rhymee was going through?

"I seek information and a private audience with the council."

"We shall give you our time after we discuss the rogues."

"Thank you," I said, gladly taking my seat.

"Let me fill you all in quickly since some of you are just now joining. You all know Red Furrin has turned a human illegally, and in turn, that human turned another. They have created a dangerous chain of combative vampires who are only loyal to Red Furrin. We know there are now ten, but soon there will be others. They have no morals, feeding upon the innocent, including women and children. Even though our ways, our rules were created for a reason, these rogues disregard them!"

"How do we put an end to the problem?" eagerly asked a vampire from behind me. "One has fed upon a little boy in my town. She disposed of his body by throwing it in a ravine. His parents are devastated. He was their life."

"State your name," ordered Mary Warren.

"Brian O'Malley, ma'am."

"We must capture them and bring them here. The rudiment shall be forced upon each and every one of them," answered Egan in response to O'Malley's question.

"Now that you all are in attendance, you all shall not leave until we have your names," said Chris Cornwell. "You see the five hundred are on record. If you are not on the list, we shall consider you a spy."

I turned and noticed a couple of vampires were now posted at the exit.

"I am no spy!" defended O'Malley.

"Of course not." Frost laughed. "If you were, you would no longer be here."

The meeting went on for several hours. Each vampire in attendance stood, stated his or her name, spoke of the atrocities witnessed, and offered help.

I was extremely concerned by this new problem we faced, but I had no time for it. I had to get back to Rhymee as soon as possible. Unless she received another bite, she would die. A third bite would mutate her skin and bones into an indestructible form, and the magic would heal any wounds inflicted upon her from that point forward. Her soul would remain permanently housed within her youthful body.

"It was nice seeing you, Thad. I grow tired of this meeting and shall take my leave. I am sure we will cross paths again," said Illissa, walking off while the others were still deliberating.

"But—"

"What?" She stopped and turned.

"They are dangerous," I pointed out.

"So am I." She smiled deviously then walked away.

No one tried to stop her.

That was rude of her, I thought. Rhymee would never just get up and walk out of a room without giving an explanation.

"You all know what to do! It is time to take action! We are running out of time! This is our last meeting until the next full moon. If you are just joining us, see Mary after the meeting. She will instruct you further. I, along with the other council members, shall help hunt these loathsome parasites!" said Frost, dismissing everyone.

The vampires filed out one by one until I only remained.

"Thadacus, take a walk with Egan and me. Haygen, Chris, Floyd, Mary, you all may go."

The other council members gathered their notes and left.

"I desire the forest," said Frost. "What about you, Braun?"

"Sounds good," replied Egan while gesturing I join them.

I wanted to confront Egan.

"I would love to join you, but may I have a moment alone with Braun?" I asked Frost.

"Of course, I will wait outside," said Frost, leaving the room.

Egan waited to speak until Frost was well gone. "I know what you are going to say. I suppose you're wondering why I am here, and I can guess by the looks you gave me you are furious with me."

"How could you allow me to think you have been dead this whole time?"

For a moment, Egan was dead quiet and detached.

"Well, I am waiting for an explanation."

"You have a right to be angry, but I was only trying to protect you from being hurt later. I will go through the Rudiment after we have wiped out the rogues."

"I could have used your help, but I suppose it just was not that important."

"Thadacus, I do not expect you to understand my choices, but if it is any consolation, I am glad to see you again."

"It does not matter anymore anyway. I have more important things to worry with."

"You know I will help you in any way I can."

"I came here to see Frost, not you," I said venomously.

Egan just sighed.

We left the room and hurried back through the passageways. Neither of us said a word until we had exited the mine, and I was not about to be the one to break the silence.

Upon tasting the fresh air, I was reminded of my growing hunger.

Frost was waiting for us to join him at the tunnel's mouth. "It's nice to finally meet you, Goodridge. The vampires are lucky to have your friend Braun with us. He is quite skilled in many things and is needed to help bring Furrin and his followers to justice. We have unsuccessfully hunted him for years."

"Now, talk to us. Who is it you seek to turn? Is it the child you discovered years ago?" asked Egan. He was irritatingly clairvoyant, and he didn't seem at all bothered by the fact that I was angry with him.

"It is. I know we are currently beyond our limits, and I would never ask a vampire to die in her stead. Understand, I do not ask this because I love her. She is truly unique, holding special gifts. I know her well. If taught, she would follow our ways. She is good."

"Why is she special? What gifts do you refer to?" asked Frost.

"She sees things others do not. She is aware of how every living thing on earth contributes and understands their functions. I am blind compared to her. I made a mistake in biting her. When she was a child, I assumed she was afraid of fictional things created by her own mind. She became introverted to an extreme and spent most every night in living terror, so I bit her, knowing the magic would help her see the world for what it really was, but my bite had the opposite effect," I said.

"How so?" asked Egan.

"Our magic only helped confirm her fears. I have felt a presence lurking underground and in the sky around her home. Something haunts her, but I am blind to it."

I did not want to fill either of them in on Rhymee's dreams or what I witnessed in the field.

"I believe you," said Egan.

"In my time as a vampire, I have only read about one type of wraith that haunts humans. I fear she is tortured by a mercuride," said Frost.

I acted like I did not know what Frost was talking about to protect Egan. Why was I inclined to protect him after what he had pulled? I suppose I was still his loyal friend, even though he had not shown me the same respect.

"I agree. Do you think she has invited them into her life?" asked Egan.

"Absolutely not!" I quickly defended.

"I will share something with you, Thadacus Goodridge, not many of our kind have the pleasure of knowing. Not only because I believe you but also because I feel you serve some greater purpose," said Frost, pausing to peer through the darkness. "Sorry. I had to make sure we are alone, and I believe we are."

Egan sniffed the air. "It is safe to talk."

"Do you swear to keep what I am about to speak of to yourself, sharing the knowledge with no other?" asked Frost.

"I swear, but why do you feel I serve a greater purpose?"

"I know how you came to vampirism. I feel you were sent back to us for some reason."

"I agree," Egan interjected.

"Vampires and humans who know of our existence often ponder upon how our kind came into being. Humans know earth was not created for us. Because of a vampire's thirst for blood, humans have created fictional stories of how we sprang from hell and how we are nothing but pure evil. We are innately human. However, our magic does come from another realm, but make no mistake, it is not hell." Frost was amused, taking a moment to chuckle.

Egan laughed with him for a moment.

"There is a realm called Lethun. Many creatures reside there, but unlike earth, the inhabitants of Lethun are immortal. Death is not forced upon the creatures of that world. They rarely see new life. Only when they choose to give up the magic housed within their bodies do they create versions of their former selves. Unlike earth, Lethun is a peaceful world. There are no wars, no famines, and no disease. They have no reason to fight because they still hold everything that was given to them since the beginning of their existence. Do not ask me when their realm was created or why. I do not know the answer," said Frost, sounding disappointed.

I was astonished yet relieved to learn I was no demon and that the magic consuming us did not originate from hell.

"The vampires from Lethun look nothing like us. They are really quite shocking with their brick-colored skin, orange fly eyes, and spiky green hair, which bursts upward like fire from their scalps. According to my journal, their fangs are long and not retractable, like a saber tooth tiger's. They stand on two legs like a human but can run fast on all fours, if needed," said Frost, seeming to marvel at the thought of their appearance. "They are what we call full bloods, although they have no desire or need to drink blood," explained Frost.

"They don't have to feed?" I asked.

"The rules of earth do not apply to the rules of Lethun. The creatures of that realm do not pull energy from plants and animals to survive, hence no famines. A blue star known as Hazure shines continually upon Lethun. No other planets, satellites, or stars shine in that realm because there is no solar system or planet orbiting the sun. Half their world remains in perpetual darkness while the other half remains in perpetual light. Lethun's inhabitants believe this star gives them what they need in all things, rejuvenating them, so they give thanks to the star by holding ceremonies in its honor.

"I know Egan has told you a little bit about the mercurides, but he has not told you everything," said Frost, taking on a humorless tone.

I gave Egan a look, but he didn't seem worried. He just smiled nonchalantly. Obviously he knew he wasn't in trouble for disclosing the information to me.

"The entire race of mercurides travel once a year to the festival of Rhea, where they bask in the light of Hazure. They need this light to restore their energy, but at all other times, they reside on the dark side of Lethun, known as Muhrk, and are rarely seen by the other inhabitants.

"Though the mercurides are equipped with wings, they do not have an easy road to travel. They begin their trek from the same spot each year, but there are no trails to follow, so they may cross a different path each time. Four thousand kilometers of sheer cliff filled with loose boulders and gravel separates Muhrk from Rho, the land of light.

"Over a thousand of these creatures stop to rest along the way, perching and nesting in the many crevices dotting the expanse. During one of those stops, the mercurides' leader, Salumus, and five others, just happened to seek shelter in the cleft holding the gate between earth and Lethun. The gate, called Argent, opened, revealing our world to them.

"Salumus did not understand what he was seeing, so he ordered all the mercurides to continue on to Rho, even though they were not fully rested. They would spend what's called an eken at the festival of light, which is about the same as a month in a human's measurement of time. During that eken, Salumus and his five closest followers had time to think about what they had witnessed, and they grew less fearful with each thought. He ordered the five to keep their discovery secret from the rest. They decided to revisit the gate alone after all the other mercurides had returned to Muhrk.

"To their dismay, Argent was closed. It only opens for about a day during the spring and summer equinox. The others grew tired of being cooped up in the crevice and begged Salumus to return home, but he would not hear of it. In the end, he was rewarded for his patience and gained entrance to the realm of earth. At first, they were quite cautious and leery of this new world and returned to Muhrk with the passing of each equinox. They also continued to join the other mercurides during Rhea to revive their strength. Salumus was forced to step down as mercuride leader since he was gone so often, and one called Jardes took his place.

"Jardes suspected foul play and secretly sent a message to the leaders of Lethun, the vampires. Upon receiving Jardes's message, the vampire king, Fallon Degg, sent a deformed vampire mercenary by the name of Karnak Nhu to discover what Salumus and his five were up to."

"How was he deformed?" I asked.

"May I explain?" politely asked Egan.

"Please do." Frost nodded.

"Unlike all other vampires, he came into being with a set of wings. The vampires considered these appendages a monstrosity, and he was required to keep them hidden or covered at all times.

"Karnak Nhu was the only one in Rho who could follow the mercurides undetected, and so he did. Knowing the foul group would attend the festival of Rhea, he patiently waited and watched them from a distance. Salumus was too arrogant to think anyone would have the audacity to challenge him, so he and his followers made haste back to the gate when it was time, paying little attention to their surroundings. Needless to say, Karnak Nhu discovered Argent. He quickly returned and reported his findings to Fallon Degg. The vampires were outraged, but he could do little because of where the gate was located. Fallon ordered Karnak to keep watch over the mercurides and their activities and report to him periodically. He made several trips between the realms before he was barred," eagerly explained Egan.

"Barred? Why was he barred?" I asked.

Frost once again took over the story.

"The vile mercuride and his band watched the animals and humans of earth for over a century, studying their vulnerabilities and weaknesses. They realized earth's creatures were each and every one subject to old age and death while they were not. Salumus decided he could easily conquer our world without consequence, providing a new home for his race.

"During their one hundred fourteenth year on earth, they began to capture small animals. They would torture them to death by different fatal blows or by fire, and with that success, they moved on to humans.

"After committing countless murders, they tried to return to Muhrk to gather an army, but neither they nor Karnak Nhu were permitted entrance during the next equinox. Argent remained sealed," Frost explained.

"Was it because they had murdered?" I asked.

"Indeed it was. Apparently Argent has a defense mechanism, and it was triggered," Egan answered.

"So they were trapped here?"

"Yes, and since they no longer could return to Lethun to renew themselves under Hazure, their magic weakened. The laws of earth began to apply somewhat, and a hunger began to grow within them. They, like us, needed the nourishing blood of humans to sustain their magic, and they took it, showing mercy to none," explained Frost in a regretful tone.

"But Karnak had not murdered, had he? Why was he not permitted to return?" I asked.

"He wrote of it in his journal. He assumed it was because he was made up of the same kind of magic as the mercurides, and Argent could not distinguish between the two," said Frost.

"Where is Karnak now if he wasn't permitted to return home?"

"Karnak fell in love with a human, and she, despite his odd appearance, loved him in return. He spent years with her and guarded her against all harm, but when she began to age, he was compelled to bite her, compelled in the same way as we are. She was the first of our kind, a half blood or a vampire of earth. She was so ancient. She did not hold a last name. Humans had not yet started the process of giving full names or distinguishing bloodlines. She was simply known as Jigh."

"The catacombs were named after her, right?" I asked.

"Correct, and by the time she became a vampire, she could speak and write in their language. Karnak taught her every-thing he knew. They too had to hunt like the mercurides, but they used discretion, only feeding upon the mortally wounded or humans who killed without cause or pity.

"For centuries, during each and every equinox, the mercu-rides attempted to leave earth, but each and every time their attempt failed, so eventually they tested the door less and less until they gave up all hope of returning to Muhrk," explained Frost, pausing to laugh.

"What is funny?" I asked, not understanding his thoughts.

"It's just…Karnak lived among the mercurides for centu-ries, and they never knew he was there." He snickered.

"He and Jigh continued to watch the gate and noticed the mercurides no longer returned, so they boldly walked up to Argent one day. Much to their surprise, they were permitted to enter. They waited in the crevice on the other side until the gate closed, making sure no mercuride had followed. He speculates in his journal that Jigh may have confused the gate because she had not tried to use it before. Sensing her goodness, it let them pass."

"So what happened to them? How did we come into being?"

"They were not greeted with open arms by the vampire monarchy. Fallon Degg was not only angered by Karnak Nhu's long absence, but he and the full bloods viewed Jigh as an atrocity, a sacrilege. After a lengthy trial, they were both sentenced to Alka Treeah, which in their language means 'the return of magic to the great one.' In our language, it means death. They also perform a ceremony. It takes the light of Hazure from a body and returns it to the star.

"Karnak was mortified as he and Jigh were chained and led to a holding chamber. He did not fear returning to Hazure but could not bear the guilt he felt for having caused Jigh's death. She tried to console him by explaining she had chosen her path, and if she had been on earth, she would have died ages back, but it was of no use. Karnak loved her too much.

"Another vampire of low stature by the name of Nork Oceen came to check on them. He held the key to their prison. Karnak knew him well—they were friends. Nhu did not want to place his friend in danger by asking for his aid, but he felt there was no other way to help Jigh. He begged his friend, and finally Nork gave in. They came up with an elaborate scheme to fool the full bloods into thinking Jigh had special powers and had escaped against Oceen's will. Karnak had to stay behind to make the story believable.

"Karnak gave Jigh his journal, instructing her to return to earth. He told her to create another vampire so she would not be alone. He explained it was the way to keep his magic alive. He also warned her to stay away from the gate so the mercurides would not gain entrance, and without his knowledge, its location would remain hidden from all of Lethun. He then bid her farewell.

"According to her journal, Oceen had to scold her to make her leave. She also described the journey home as a difficult one. She had to climb down the same steep cliffs the mercurides and Karnak had traveled up and down with wings. In her history, she describes being lost for, she thinks, approximately ten human years. In that time, she hid from the mercurides during their annual journey."

"What did she eat?" I asked, remembering I too needed to feed.

"She discovered a small birdlike animal, called a yar, and sucked the magic from its veins. She found she only needed to feed upon a few. That magic sustained her much longer than a human's blood did here on earth.

"Over time, she had sought shelter in so many nooks strewn across the cliffs that the memory of the one holding the gate left her. She describes herself as crazy, and she was considering showing herself to the mercurides the very next time they traveled up the cliffs, but luck was on her side. She was sitting quietly in the entryway to the gate, reading Karnak's journal for comfort, when the gate opened. She wasted no time in leaping back to earth.

"To her surprise, upon her return, Salumus and his band were no more. They had been destroyed, but by what she did not know. Later, she discovered their essence or spirits remained, but they were powerless to anyone.

"For centuries she lived alone. No human could compare to Karnak Nhu. One day while hunting, the scent of blood led her to a man tied to a tree. His skin had been sliced deeply every few inches to draw blood to the surface, yet the cuts were shallow enough to keep him alive. He would not make an acceptable offering dead. Out of the six straws to choose from, he drew the short one. He was a druid priest and went along with the sacrifice willingly. He was content to give his life to the harvest goddess so his people could produce ample crops.

"He wailed out in pain in hopes of calling her to him. When he laid his eyes upon Jigh, he thought he had succeeded. He invited Jigh to take his life in the name of his people, and at first, Jigh was going to accept his offer, but something stopped her," said Frost.

"What?" I asked with great interest.

"She saw strength in that man, not only physically but also mentally. She was compelled to pass on Karnak's magic for the first time, so instead of killing him, she bit him. His wounds rapidly healed as she carried him away to her dwelling. He did not try to escape because in his mind he belonged to her. She bit him a second and third time, and he became the second of our kind," explained Frost with pride.

"Who was he? What was his name?" I asked, hoping I had met him at some point in time.

"He passed his magic to me and made me vampire," said Egan. "I have spoken of Dario before."

I put my head down in regret. I would never have the pleasure of meeting him. He had been gone for quite some time.

"I wish he were here too." Egan placed his hand on my shoulder.

"To answer your question, we do not know why the mercurides keep a vigilant watch on your girl. We know nothing more than what we have told you," stated Frost. "And as for your request…"

Here it came, the moment I was to decide whether I truly hated or liked Frost. I knew no matter what his intention was, if he denied my request, he would forever remain one of my enemies.

"Understand I usually break the rules for no one. In the chaotic state we are in now, it is especially a bad idea, but after speaking to you and learning of Rhymee's abilities, I am going to grant your request. For some reason, I feel her destiny is intertwined with ours," said Frost compassionately.

"Thank you," I said to the both of them. "I will keep my word. The conversation this evening did not happen."

"No, it happened. Just do not talk about it." Frost laughed lightheartedly. "Now, I grow hungry. Do you care to join us, Thadacus, before you return?"

"I will find something on my journey back. I don't really have time to hunt," I declined graciously.

"I hope the two of you attend our next meeting. I should like to meet Rhymee," suggested Egan.

"I will, if at all possible," I said.

Suddenly I felt as if the wind had been knocked out of me and a ball of invisible fire burned in my gut. Grabbing my stomach, I bent in half, rent with pain.

"What is wrong?" asked Frost, alarmed.

Egan grabbed my shoulder and helped pull me up.

"It's…Rhymee! She's been hurt!" I gasped.

"How badly?" asked Egan.

"I don't know if I can make it back to her in time," I said, losing focus while anger replaced my pain.

"You are going to need your strength to return quickly. Come with me. I can help you," said Frost.

Within moments, we were again down in the tunnels, this time taking a different route. Frost took out a chain of skeleton keys and unlocked a large iron door. Inside were small cubic prison cells. They were all empty save one.

"This one murdered his wife and unborn child. He was angry she had gotten pregnant and accused her of infidelity. He beat her till she was unconscious and then drowned her. She now rests at the bottom of Lake of the Woods never to be found," explained Frost, full of hate.

"You can't prove anything!" the prisoner lashed out. "You have captured an innocent man! Who are you people anyway?"

Frost ignored his question and pleas.

"I was hoping to torture him slowly before devouring him, but he is now your gift," said Frost, handing me the keys.

Upon hearing this, the prisoner's eyes grew wide with terror.

"You can question him first if you would like," suggested Egan. "I know it is hard taking one without hunting him down and discerning his transgressions beforehand. You need to know he is guilty."

"Come closer," I softly ordered.

The prisoner hesitated.

"Now!" I said sternly.

He slowly walked toward me. When he was close enough, I grabbed his shirt and pulled him tightly against the bars of his cell.

"Look into my eyes, and tell me you did not murder your wife," I bid, seeking the truth.

For a split second, he lowered his eyes in guilt and had to muster the courage to lie to me.

"I did not murder my wife and child!" he said with hatred.

I let him go, and he quickly ran and cowered in the corner.

"We will leave the two of you alone then," said Frost, gesturing for Egan to follow him.

"Travel safely, my friend. I assume you know the way out," said Egan.

"Promise me you will spend one more day with me before you go through with the rudiment," I requested.

"I promise, but it cannot be at my old estate. I don't want Savora to know I still live."

"Agreed. I will not mention that I have seen you," I promised.

"I will look forward to our visit," he said, and then he turned and left.

I walked over to the cell and unlocked it.

"So you are going to kill me for no reason!" he yelled while tears streamed from his face.

"There is no time to argue over this. There is always a consequence for one's actions, whether it is here or in the afterlife," I calmly said, walking toward him.

He swiftly grabbed a medium-sized rock that was lying near him and attempted to bash my skull in with it. He was stunned when it had no effect.

"Good. I like a strong fight," I said.

"How did—"

"I will let you in on a little secret. I am a vampire," I said, exposing my fangs.

He screamed while grabbing my shoulders and attempting to push me back but to no avail.

I took my time feeding, draining him completely.

Frost was right. I would need my strength for the journey back.

INTRUDER

I woke to a beautiful summer's day, but I couldn't really enjoy it. The light hurt my eyes, but at night I could hear further and see clearer than ever. I lay in bed for almost an hour, listening to my family enjoy breakfast and bustle around the house. Everyone knew better than to disturb me on the weekends, lest it put me in a foul mood for the entire day. I wasn't a morning person.

I finally decided to get up and go to the kitchen. I could hear running water, scraping, dishes clanging, and strokes of the broom. *Good, they are cleaning up. I will just eat a bowl of instant oatmeal*, I thought, sliding on my slippers and robe.

"You're up! I saved you a plate of waffles," said Mom while focused on scrubbing a cast-iron skillet.

"Thanks, Mom," I said, grabbing the maple syrup.

Dad walked back in the kitchen.

"Forgot my thermos of coffee," he said.

"Morning, Dad."

"Good morning! Your sisters and I are putting new salt blocks out for the cows. Want to join us?" he asked. Dad really didn't need my help; he just missed spending time with me.

"Sure. Sounds fun."

"Well, take your time and finish your breakfast. I need to load the salt and get Old Green going."

"I'll be out in a few minutes."

Dad was smiling as he walked out. He forgot his coffee again.

I barely chewed the waffles, swallowing in massive bites. My mom made the best waffles, but today the most enjoyable part of breakfast was my tall glass of orange juice with pulp. The blast of cold citrus hit the spot.

"Rhymee, he will wait on you! It's not good for you to chew so quickly," Mom said, annoyed I wasn't taking time to appreciate her cooking. "You still look a little pale and undernourished. If it weren't for your vibrant eyes, I would still think you were ill. Would you like me to fry you some turkey bacon really quickly? You can take it with you."

"Mom, I feel fine. The waffles were really good and filling. I couldn't eat bacon right now. I'm too full," I said, downing the last of my orange juice.

"Well, at least the orange juice will do you some good."

I started to carry my plate and glass to the sink.

"I got it. Go join your dad and sisters," she said.

I ran to my room, threw on some shorts, grabbed a cheap pair of sunglasses, and then raced outside. I stopped on the sidewalk for a moment to enjoy the warm breeze. Abruptly, the wind picked up, shaking the oaks and maples in the front yard. It seemed like the wind couldn't make up its mind as to which direction it wanted to blow. It changed directions every few seconds. At first, I didn't think anything of the wind, but when the trees suddenly began to shed their vibrant-green summer leaves, I worried. Not one stick or branch had fallen along with the leaves, and the leaf tips were all facing east.

"I forgot my coffee, honey. I will meet you at the truck," said Dad, walking up the lane.

I didn't say anything. I was too distracted by what had just happened.

"What in the world?" he asked, noticing the pile of leaves blanketing the ground. "Rhymee, do you know what caused this?"

I didn't respond.

"Rhymee!"

"Sorry, Dad, a strong wind. Have you seen the leaves do this before?" I asked, hoping he would say yes.

He studied the ground and sky for a moment.

"I can't say that I have. What I find the oddest is that they only fell here. Look over there and at the rest of the yard." He pointed.

I instinctively knew the wind and leaves were a warning. I gathered, after much thought, that a danger approached from the east. Was it the red cloud? It had been powerless before, but what if it had changed? I made a decision to prepare myself; I wasn't going to be caught off guard.

I loaded up with my sisters in the back of the old truck. It was an unusual treat to get to ride back there without seatbelts. Our parents would never have let us ride that way on a major highway.

"Hey, Rhymee, do you want a fudgesicle?" asked Rhondel, rapidly biting chunks out of one.

"No, thanks," I said. I was still trying to figure out why the leaves had fallen the way they had. What did it mean?

"What's wrong?" asked Rhegan, picking up on my mood.

"Nothing. I just don't feel like ice cream this early."

"Ready, girls?" asked Dad, quickly walking to the cab with his thermos.

"Yep!" said Rhegan excitedly.

We tossed a couple heavy salt blocks in the field while Dad slowly drove and inspected his and Aunt Hada's cows.

When we were finished, Rhondel and I rested on the fenders while Rhegan sat on the bed of the truck.

"Everything seems to be in order. Are you girls ready to head back? Mom probably has lunch fixed."

"Yep, we're thirsty," said Rhegan.

"Yeah, I want one of those grape sodas Mom bought," said Rhondel, licking her chapped lips.

Dad put the truck in four-wheel drive and slowly drove up the steep, rocky hill to the gate.

"Okay, Rhegan, can you open it up for us?" he shouted out the window.

Rhegan leapt over the side of the truck.

"Yeah, one of those sodas does sound goo—" I stopped midsentence when I looked up to find the cows had all grouped into the shape of an arrow facing east, like a flock of birds.

Detecting my shock, Rhondel placed her hand over her brow to block the harsh rays of the sun and peered in the same direction as me.

"Am I seeing things?" she asked in disbelief.

"Probably," I responded. I didn't want to explain my suspicions.

"Rhegan and I are here to help," she said, unexpectedly seeming like she was in a trance.

"What?" I asked, confused by my sister's sudden offer. "Help with what?"

Rhondel was staring blankly out into the valley.

"Rhondel, what did you mean?" I asked, finding my sister's behavior scary. I was supposed to be the weird one, not her.

"What?" she asked, seeming dazed.

"Never mind. Do you think Mom and Dad will take us to a movie this afternoon?" I asked, changing the subject.

"That's a great idea! I'll ask when we get to the house!"

The cows had moved on, but I was still trying to think of a plan. I knew something was coming, but I didn't know what or when. All I could do was try to defend myself because I didn't know when Thad would return.

Little did I know that the strange car I had spotted up the road meant danger. A stranger watched us pull up to the garage. She had been parked there all morning. We were oblivious to her intentions.

"Rhymee, are you sure you don't want to come along? I heard this movie is a good one," asked Dad, right before joining Mom, Rhondel, and Rhegan in the car.

"I really want to read this new book I bought. I will enjoy it more than a movie," I said, eagerly holding up a thick paperback. "You guys go. I'll be okay. If I need anything, I will call Aunt Hada."

"But it was your idea we go to the movies!" Rhondel pointed out. She had hoped I would come because she hadn't gotten to do anything fun with me since my illness.

Mom and Dad both gave me a suspicious look.

"I changed my mind. I would have to take a shower, and you guys are ready. I'd make you late. Rhondel, how about this evening we make some chocolate chip cookies?"

"Oh, that sounds great," Rhegan interjected.

Rhondel looked at me reluctantly for a moment. "You promise?"

"Of course!"

"Well, then we're off," said Dad.

I watched my parents pull away, and then I ran inside, grabbed a footstool, and climbed on top of the kitchen counter beside the refrigerator. I knew Dad kept his extra set of gun cabinet keys hidden away there.

I darted up the stairs, opened the cabinet, and pulled out the twelve-gauge shotgun. The box of shells for it was sitting on a small shelf above the rack.

I was not intimidated by the weapon. Dad had taken me to target practice with him a few years ago, so I had a feel for the gun and a surprisingly good aim.

I knew Dad wouldn't miss the gun for a while since he rarely went hunting. He just didn't enjoy hunting as much as he did when he was younger. The thought of killing, even for the necessity of meat, turned his gut.

I cautiously carried the gun down the stairs and laid it on a small, wooden bench in the kitchen. My stomach was growling ferociously. It was dusk, and I hadn't eaten since breakfast.

I'll eat and then hide the gun under my bed. I still have a little time before Mom and Dad return, I thought, finding a cold plate of chicken in the refrigerator.

As I was about to take my first bite, someone knocked on the kitchen door.

I was reluctant to answer. I found it odd the stranger had not tried the front door first.

I looked out the kitchen window and saw a blonde woman, approximately in her forties, wearing a headscarf and an out-of-style dress standing on the steps. She seemed distraught about something, and she was holding a water jug.

I took a deep breath and glanced at the gun.

"Hello? Is anyone home?" the stranger yelled through the door's windowpane in a desperate, sweet voice. "I think my radiator is overheating and needs water!"

Mom and Dad would be ashamed if I didn't help her. I'm crazy for thinking she is some kind of monster, I thought, taking a second look.

The lady turned and slowly started to walk away, holding her head down in disappointment.

"Can I help you?" I shouted, pulling the yellow curtain back on the door but keeping it locked.

The stranger's eyes lit up as she quickly whirled back around.

"Oh, my dear, thank goodness you're home! My name is Hazel Mirerott. My car broke down up the road, and if I don't get some water, I'm going to be stranded out here in the middle of nowhere."

"If water is all you need, there is a hydrant on the side of the house."

"I could be wrong you know—it may be the engine. Can your dad come and take a look?"

"Why don't you try the water first, and if your car still doesn't start, you can come back," I suggested through the glass, not wanting to give away any information.

"Oh, I am sorry. He isn't here, is he? How long do you think it will be? You see, my son is at home with a young sitter, and I am worried. I told her I would be back by dark, and I am obviously not going to meet that deadline."

"Not long," I said coldly, getting the feeling the woman was prying.

"Well, I appreciate your time, my dear. You can go back to watching your shows."

I lifted an eyebrow, slightly smiled at the kooky woman, and then nodded. I didn't feel like explaining to a stranger that I rarely watched television.

I turned back to the gun. I had to find a way to get it to my bedroom before my parents returned, but I would have to wait for the stranger to leave. I would have to unlock the kitchen door to reach my bedroom door. There was not a connecting door from my renovated bedroom to inside the house. If all else failed and my parents returned before the lady left,

I would hide the gun under the couch in the living room and retrieve it later.

I sat down at the kitchen table and took a chuck out of a chicken leg then washed it down with a big chug of orange juice.

Creak!

I was suddenly alarmed. It sounded like someone had stepped on the only noisy, wooden floorboard in the living room. I knew the sound well. I stopped chewing and listened intently.

I am imagining things, I thought, but I lost my appetite. I stood up with my plate and peered out the window as I dumped my chicken bones in the garbage, and then I stepped to the refrigerator to put away the juice. I looked up and saw the woman standing in the entryway to the kitchen. I gasped with fear.

"What the…? How did…?"

"I let myself in, dear," said Hazel in her sweet voice, but her gaze was evil.

"I can't help you with your car. My parents will be here any time."

"Then I don't have time for pleasantries, so I'll make this quick," said Hazel, pulling a long, thin knife from the belt around her dress.

I raced for the gun, and as I did, Hazel threw the knife. It lodged deep in my back, and I screamed in agony.

I turned for only a moment and saw her coming toward me, pulling out a second knife from behind her back. I knew I had to reach the gun. The look in the stranger's eyes told me she intended to slit my throat.

"That was a good throw, but it won't quite do the trick," explained the depraved woman nonchalantly.

She hadn't noticed the twelve-gage lying on the bench, so she took her time, leisurely strolling toward me.

With the last strength I had, I reached the gun, picked it up, pointed it at Hazel, and I pulled the trigger.

I don't know how much time had passed, but I could hear the footsteps and voices of my family. I desperately wanted to call to them, but I couldn't.

Rhondel and Rhegan came bounding around the corner to the kitchen door, carrying bags of groceries.

"And you're not going to eat all the chips before we get the cookie dough done. Hurry up! This is heavy," griped Rhegan.

"I am! I can't see the keyhole," said Rhondel, trying to unlock the door.

"Well, here comes Mom and Dad with the rest. Let them get it," said Rhegan, setting her bag on the ground.

"Ah ha! Got it!" said Rhondel, rushing in with her face practically glued to the brown, paper bag.

Rhondel tripped over a huge lump in the floor, me, spilling her sack of groceries.

"And I will have you know, I will eat as many chips as—"Rhegan looked down to see what had caused her sister's fall and instantly began screaming.

Mom and Dad dropped their bags and sprinted to my sisters.

"Dad, Rhymee!" shouted Rhondel, pointing to the ground.

Rhegan was holding my hand, tears streaming down her face.

"Bhren, call 911!" ordered Dad, kneeling and pressing his fingers to my neck. "Hurry! She has a pulse!"

"Don't touch her! You might make things worse!" snapped Mom, holding for the operator.

"Girls, get back! Go to the other room!"

"Yes, I need an ambulance immediately! My daughter's been stabbed!" cried Mom hysterically. I wanted to tell her I was there with her, but I didn't have the strength.

Twenty minutes later, red and white lights flashed through the darkness; the ambulance had arrived, followed shortly by the cops.

"If the movie hadn't been sold out, we wouldn't have made it back to her in time." Mom shuddered right before stepping up in the ambulance.

"I need to talk to the cops and drop the girls off at Hada's, and then I'm right behind you!"

"Hurry, Richard! I can't bear this alone!"

"We think the front door lock was picked," I could hear an officer say.

"Did you see anyone leave, Mr. Stewart?" asked a hefty, muscular officer named Rance.

"No one. Who could have done this? Why?" choked Dad.

"We will do our best to find the answers to those questions. We've got help on the way," reassured the officer.

That was all I could remember before the ambulance doors slammed shut.

A STARTLING VISIT

The magic surging through Rhymee's veins called to me. It desperately warned me of her peril and led me in a straight line to Ervington Medical Center rather than the farm.

Stinking visiting hours, I thought as I paced back and forth in the waiting room. The nursing staff and other visitors didn't question my reason for being there; they assumed I was worrying over a sick relative, like they all were. I kept my eyes closed and my head down, occasionally sitting and then standing.

A nurse walked in. "Would anyone like some coffee?"

I shook my head. Nobody in the room wanted coffee. Their nerves were already shot without adding caffeine to their stress.

Hours passed. The room slowly emptied until only I remained.

The nurse came in and began to pick up magazines that were scattered around the area.

"Sir, I'm afraid you will need to return tomorrow. Visiting hours are over," she kindly pointed out.

I nodded that I understood, and then I left. I made my way to the elevator, but rather than hitting the lobby button, I hit the one leading to ICU on the third floor.

A nurse sat at a dimly lit station. I gently breathed. It didn't take much. Her face plunged into a stack of papers. She was out. One more to go and then no one stood between me and Rhymee. Richard was already asleep in the recliner next to his daughter, but I filled the room with my intoxicating breath. I did not want him waking until I was ready.

I rushed over to Rhymee and wasted no time. I carefully lifted her, exposing her neck.

"What are you doing here?" asked a mellow voice, startling me from behind.

I angrily whirled around to find the same nurse that had offered coffee in the waiting room, poking her head around the door.

"Well, I asked you a question," she said, paying no attention to my odd appearance.

It took a moment for me to realize she was not human. Her black hair had an unusual sheen, and her golden eyes sparkled in the dim light. She smelled like, how do I put it, like boiling citrus. What an odd smell. No blood coursed through her veins, and she certainly was not vampire. Then it struck me. I had heard her voice before. It was her whispering to me through the darkness, urging me to feed the night Rhymee ran from me at the pond.

"What are you?" I asked impatiently.

"I could ask you the same thing," she stated, entering the room.

"Are you an agent of death, come for Rhymee?" I asked, hesitating to threaten her.

She grinned.

I stood guard. She would not get past me.

"I need to have a word with you, Thadacus. Do not fear. I will not come between you and the girl," she said, leaning against one of the walls. "I assure you she will last while I speak."

"What do you need?" I asked, distrusting her purpose. "How do you know me?"

"I know lots of things, Thadacus Goodridge. Although I am ancient, I am not immortal like you. Some of the knowledge I carry has been passed down to me from my grandparents, to my parents, and then to me. You see, unlike you, I am bound to the laws of earth."

"What is your point? If you know me, you know I do not willingly hold conversations with total strangers, especially those who rudely interrupt me, human or not," I said.

"You cannot turn this girl without paying a horrible consequence," she whispered.

"If you try to stop me, I will kill you."

"Do you know why the dark spirits are after her? I do," she said playfully, seeming to know I would want to know more.

"I'm listening."

"She is a descendant from an ancient tribe that destroyed the bodies of six mercurides that are now trapped in this realm. Only their magical essence remains. That is why they harbor ill will toward her, and her family too for that matter."

"How could humans kill such powerful creatures?" I asked.

"Her ancient ancestors were called Gauls by the Romans. Later they became known as Celts and are involved with the Iron Age. However, long before the Romans gave them a name, Rhymee's tribe knew the secrets of earth, and they were natural warriors. Individually they often excelled, becoming scholars, healers, soldiers, and a number of other things. When they joined together, they were an unstoppable force. They would fight death to the very end, ignoring the pain to prove their strength. The ancient ones knew they held the secret of the cosmos. The mercurides' invasion crisis caused Rhymee's ancestors of the great Celtic warriors to reawaken. Their power and destinies were revealed.

"The mercurides killed and killed. Their lust for blood grew with each slaying, not because they needed to feed but because they desired inflicting pain and cruelty upon the weak. Many animals were forced into extinction during that time. Only a handful of humans scattered across the earth remained, and they lived in constant fear. Salumus and his band traveled far, but it was many centuries before they came into Gaul territory. During this time, the tribe was small and had not yet spread. They lived in the cold, secluded forests of what is now Britain and were not known to the rest of the world. When the mercurides entered their land, they were fearless of the task ahead."

I thought of Karnak Nhu and Jigh; the battle must have occurred while she was lost in Lethun.

"My kind believes earth heard the cries of the slain, so they called the Gauls to battle."

"Why them? Why do the Gauls alone possess this strength?" I asked.

"They are considered sacred to my people. They inherit the gift. It is their birthright."

"What has this got to do with Rhymee? Why can't she become a vampire? There could be no one more innocent!" I defended.

"The only reason she, her ancestors, and anyone carrying the Gaul blood can possess such strength and power is because they are mortal. If given a vampire's abilities, they could destroy anything or anyone. Their knowledge currently sleeps, but it is limitless. We fairies have seen the ones who carry the blood go to war. After fighting for so long, they cannot reverse the effects. They crave the thrill of battle. It is as if they carry an invisible sword within them. Its blade constantly cuts at their insides, even when they are children. Once this sword is used, there is no putting it down. My kind believes it is better for them to die in battle, for if they do not, they become tortured. It is why she became sick long before old age. Her blood struggles against your magic because it is forbidden for one of her lineage to hold the power of this realm and another."

"What great powers do they possess?" I asked, doubting the Gauls could be more powerful than vampires.

"It sounds so simple really, but their will is a force to be reckoned with. If they want a mountain moved, they will find a way to make it happen. They often inherit a natural talent for using weaponry. Through the centuries, they have taken deathblows but will fight till their last breath leaves them, ignoring the pain. They can also read and understand earth's warnings, like your girl did the morning before she was attacked," she said, glancing to the bed.

"It is forewarned in our writings. If ever given enough time, these sacred humans could learn to control things like metals and even pure energy. You have been told that you are indestructible, but if she becomes vampire, she could kill you without hesitation. There would be no need of a ceremony."

"Rhymee could never kill out of cruelty or become a tyrant," I argued.

"You know a vampire's magic will awaken that which is asleep. She has already begun to see things in a different light. Your girl picked up the hilt of her sword long ago and cannot put it down. I have watched her for a long time. She has the heart of a lion. Do not provoke that which you do not understand. You have been sickened by her blood already. Can you recall its bitter taste?"

I looked away. I could not argue the point.

"It is like in nature when a bird preys upon a poisonous insect or butterfly. The insect's taste is a warning. Do not ignore this one, Thadacus Goodridge, for another bite could poison you to death."

"Who are you?" I asked with abhorrence to the news she bore.

She folded her arms. "I am called Sighka, and I am a fairy. Don't you believe in fairies?"

Dang it, why does this always happen to me, I thought. *The strange, the odd, never fails to beckon at my door.*

I studied her eyes. They were unwavering, seeming to dare me to challenge her story. She was crafty, but I felt she told the truth.

"Why have you not made yourselves known to us before now?"

"Have you not read about us?" she asked in a condescending tone. "However, it is easy for us to hide. We can look like anything we wish. Shape-shifting is one of our talents."

"I have read fictional fairy stories."

"And I have read fictional vampire stories, yet here you stand. We do not want others to know about us because we are so different. The human race would hunt us down and kill us. Am I not right?" she asked.

"Then why do you trust showing yourself to me?" I asked.

"Because you are not a human anymore, and it was necessary so I could deliver my message. I do take a risk in coming here this night," she explained with a hint of fear. "I trust you, Thadacus Goodridge. I have watched you for a long time."

"No matter what you say, I am going to save her," I cautioned.

"Do not misunderstand my reasons. I am not here to stop you. This decision rests on your shoulders. I am a mere messenger," she said innocently, but I felt there was some ulterior motive.

I turned and quickly looked at Rhymee with new respect. She appeared even more beautiful, and I suddenly felt the urge again to turn her but not for the reason of saving her. I wanted to witness what she would become.

"How do you know she carries this blood?"

"We have watched the Gauls and their descendants since the beginning of their time."

"Why do Rhymee's sisters not behave in the same way? Why can't they see the mercurides?"

"Rhymee's parents are both descendants from two of the most powerful Gaul families. Rhymee is firstborn, so she naturally inherits the role of protector. We fairies think it is odd Rhymee could have such a strong connection with nature and the magical forces of earth before there is a calling or need of it. No other child on earth at this moment sees things as clearly as she does. She is quite unique. It terrifies some fairies to think she could become vampire and live on," she said.

"Does it terrify you?" I asked.

"Somewhat," she replied honestly. "I must go. I have already told you too much. Please keep my warning a secret," she requested.

"If you know anything about me, you know I cannot do that. I answer to our Ragnvaldr. We are not allowed to keep secrets such as this."

"Then may your heart guide you. I will leave you with a thought. Knowing now what you do, would your vampire council still agree to turn her? Do you think they would have a problem with that?" She quietly stepped back out the door. "I must leave this torturous place. It smells like death's sweat. I need the fresh air of the forest."

As she left, I stood there like a stone, showing no emotion, giving no response, but inside terror gripped me. I remembered the painful sickness I had fought in the well. I knew I would have to swallow the blood again to turn Rhymee. Could I overcome another dose, or would it destroy me? I knelt down beside her bed and stared at her. I marveled at her strengths as a natural warrior but also her vulnerabilities as a human.

She coughed, and then she gasped for air. I suddenly panicked. Had I run out of time?

THE CHOICE

Richard had requested blanket after blanket, but the hospital blankets were thin, and they were not doing any good. Rhymee was cold. Her lips and fingertips had turned light blue. The repetitious noises from the beeping heart monitor and the IV drip were annoying. I wanted to rip them from her body and the walls. Sorrow crushed me as memories of her as a child riding her bike and playing with her sisters flooded my mind, and then I thought of myself for a moment and of what I would have to give up if I bit her a third time. The answer was life; her blood would poison me to death. I had died before and had no memory of what was next. Could I give up my existence for her? I knew the answer, so I wasted no more time.

I turned and looked at Richard sleeping in the chair, and I could hear hospital staff moving around on other floors. It was impossible to turn her in this place. We would be exposed.

I felt trapped. How could we leave the hospital unnoticed? I did not want to take her downstairs; too many people were coming in and out. It was not within my power to put them all to sleep. I walked over to the window, which could not be opened, and looked down to the alley below. I saw no one at that late hour. I stood there feeling helpless. *What to do?* I asked myself. Breaking the window would create a problem.

"Rhymee, I am taking you from here," I turned and whispered, but she did not respond.

Protect her wound; keep her strong, I meditated, hoping the magic inside her would obey my desire.

I pressed my forehead and hands flat against the window. I was running out of time. How could we escape? Without thinking, I began burrowing my unyielding nail into the glass out of anger and frustration until my index finger could feel the breeze outside, and then I had an idea.

At first, I didn't know if it would work, but I started to etch a huge, deep circle in the window, all the while holding the center tightly with my index finger. When I had finished, I tapped firmly around the cut glass. I felt the disk break free and pulled it inside, carefully laying it in the corner behind the recliner where no one would notice.

I wrapped Rhymee up tightly in her blankets, cradled her in my arms, and walked over to the hole I had just created. I gently hoisted her through it and laid her on the railed ledge. I crawled through next. With fresh, balmy air blowing in, I didn't have much time before the effects of my breath would wear off and Richard would wake.

While keeping slight pressure on the wound in her back, I lifted my love, stepped over the black metal railing, and then bounded to the street below.

I bulleted from side street to side street, hoping our flight would go unseen, and did not stop until we reached the protection and cover of the woods.

I halted in a cedar tree thicket. I did not want to risk going any farther with her. I took a few moments to prepare for my fate; the last time I died there was no time to reflect on the time that had been given to me. The thought of joining my father, mother, and sister gave me courage. I was ready. Death might take me, but it would not get Rhymee.

I sat down, pressing my back against a tree for support while holding her tightly. My fangs, which constantly had an itching desire to rip and gouge, warily sank into her neck. She woke from her coma and screamed out in pain, but upon recognizing my face, she became silent, not wanting to show weakness. She grabbed my arm and squeezed hard, suppressing her agony.

I concentrated on allowing my magic to flow from me to her.

Rhymee, take my light. It is what you need, I begged her with my mind.

Her blood caused my mouth and tongue to surge with pain. I had to swallow it to seal our exchange. I didn't welcome the eminent suffering, but stopping was not an option.

I could feel her human limitations beginning to pass away. One organ and body part at a time fought the magic before succumbing to its power.

I pulled my fangs from her neck and tried to keep my composure, but I slowly lost control of my muscles. The bark of the tree raked my back as I slid to the ground. I barely had the strength to hold Rhymee as I went. I could feel her blood taking hold. This time was different than the last. My entire body began to sting, including the center of my eyes. The stinging turned to burning, especially in my mouth and throat. I screamed, but there was no sound. Had my vocal cords melted away? Her pain and my own merged. It was unlike any torture I had ever known, and it did not end quickly.

Finally the pain ended in my toes and feet, and then nothingness spread up from there into my legs. My death had come. It was spreading through my limbs, knocking them out of commission, like a disease. I lost consciousness before I could tell Rhymee what she needed to know. My last thought was of sunrise and of how she would become blind and lost and all alone.

I was dazed with foggy eyesight, and someone or something had a tight hold on me and wouldn't let go. I struggled to free myself but failed. I was ready to kill whatever held me.

"You must drink more, Thadacus," a gentle voice requested.

I stopped struggling. "Rhymee?"

"You must swallow all of it, Thadacus. I know it tastes terrible, but it'll heal you," she said, holding my head gently in her arms.

I did not understand but did as she requested, and I choked down the revolting concoction. She had earned my trust long ago.

"It's okay. I won't let anything happen to you," she reassured me.

"What is in it?" I cringed at the nasty taste.

She tucked her hair behind her ears and smiled. "The main ingredient is pine sap."

"What else?"

"Crushed clover," she hesitated.

"And?"

She gulped. "You will be angry," she explained.

"I will understand. Just tell me," I sympathized.

"The tails of lightning bugs, a little creek mud, and my saliva."

"Your saliva?"

She held me tighter and gave my forehead tiny kisses.

The feeling began coming back in my limbs. I no longer felt paralyzed.

"How did you know what to give me?" I asked.

"The last thing I remember is you holding me in your arms and then the unbearable pain. I wanted to die, but I wasn't allowed to. When one section of my body found peace, another section would begin to writhe in agony. I didn't know what was happening. When the torment ended, I turned over to find you lying beside me. I shook you and pleaded with you to wake, but you didn't move. I searched the area, longing for help. I panicked."

"I am sorry, Rhymee," I said, feeling bad for having put her through that torture alone.

"A creature like no other I have ever seen heard me. She was the color of tree bark, yet there was something human about her. Her eyes were bright green. At first, I assumed she had been the one who hurt you. I demanded she explain who she was and her purpose. She started to run, but I think she knew better than to cross me at that moment. She said that you knew her, and her name's Sighka."

"She helped you!" I asked shocked.

"Who is she?" asked Rhymee. "After she told me the ingredients for the potion, she disappeared."

Why she helped us after I blatantly disregarded her message confused me. "She is a fairy. I did not know they existed until earlier this night," I slowly explained, swallowing more than usual to get rid of the bitter taste within my mouth. "Did she say why she chose to help us?"

"Was she not supposed to?"

"She told me it was forbidden to bite you, but I did not care. I could not let you go."

Rhymee quietly responded by holding me even tighter. Her skin no longer turned red when she touched me, and she did not have to give in and let go from the pain of our embrace. As soon as I could focus, I noticed her color was back. She no longer had dark circles under her eyes or blue lips, and I could not recall her eyes being a more vibrant shade of green. I was relieved to know she was all right.

"I didn't trust her, but I didn't have any other choices. I knew you were dying. She said my blood had poisoned you. Is that true, Thad?" she asked.

"She told me the same thing while you were in the hospital, but I did not care. I was willing to die with you if I could not turn you."

"Did she tell you why? What is wrong with me?" asked Rhymee.

"Yes, but it is a long story. Rhymee, what happened is not your fault. Do not beat yourself up. Anyway, I feel fine, especially right now," I said, nestling closer to her waist.

It was tempting to ignore all thoughts, except for the feeling of her soft fingers. I had not been touched in that manner in a long while, but slowly my awareness returned, and I rose with a start.

"What hour is it?"

Rhymee glanced at her watch. "Three in the morning. Why?" she asked, puzzled.

"You must return to the hospital before daybreak!"

"But they will not understand my sudden recovery."

"This is going to be difficult, Rhymee, but you must pass away in front of your father. The magic within you will do your bidding. You will not have a pulse if you so choose."

"What? Thad, my dad will go into hysterics. I don't know if I can stand to see him in so much pain." Rhymee's eyes began to glow with magical tears. "Why can't we just run away?"

I looked down because I couldn't look her in the face. I felt her sudden fear, anguish, and doubt. She did not want to see her dad suffer. I did not want to tell her no, but I knew I had to. "Rhymee, think about it. Your dad, mom, and sisters have been preparing for the worst. Your wound was fatal. Anyone else stabbed the way you were would have died. You held on only because you were partly already transforming into a vampire. If you do not return to the hospital, I fear it could cause problems for your family. Hopefully your dad still sleeps. My breath will have worn off by now, but he was sleeping on his own before I arrived."

"Thad, I don't know if I am ready for this or if I can maintain my composure while I'm pretending to be dead."

I finally gained strength enough to look at her. "Rhymee, I will help you through this. Do you trust me?"

She nodded.

"I will lead you back to the hospital, and then I will return to the farm and wait for you there. Once we arrive, clear your mind. Try to think of nothing. Since I turned you, we are mentally connected. You just have to allow our minds to link. We can communicate that way. While you are lying in the hospital bed, I will feed your emotions. As long as you remain focused on me, you will feel nothing but the love I have for you; I swear."

"How do I do that?"

"Let's practice. Close your eyes, and I will close mine." I took her by the hands. "Now, focus on me." I waited a moment, and then I spoke to her with my mind, *Can you hear me?*

"Yes," she answered out loud.

Good, say something back to me using your mind, I told her through my thoughts.

I'm terrified of what's to come, she cast back.

There is no need to be. I will protect you.

Rhymee took a deep breath and opened her eyes widely with a start. "Do you know what I'm thinking all the time?"

"Not unless you choose to link with me. If we need to communicate with each other at great distances, we can."

"But how will I know that you are trying to speak to me?"

"You will feel me brush against your conscience. Let me show you. Walk a ways off, behind those trees." I pointed. "Once you get there, think about the forest and nothing else."

"Okay," said Rhymee. She walked until she was out of sight.

I waited for a few minutes, and then I cast a question to her with my thoughts. *Are you wearing Mjollnir?*

Always, she replied.

She appeared amazed by her new telepathic powers when she stepped back into the clearing, and then she slowly walked toward me.

"Are you ready? We do not have much time."

"I guess. Let's just get it over with."

We sprinted swiftly across the countryside. I could have pushed Rhymee to run even harder, but I did not want to overwhelm her again. She had dealt with enough already, and the hardest part was yet to come. She could test her true strength another time.

When we reached the hospital, she looked up to the second-story window then at me skeptically.

"Rhymee, you can jump that far without making a sound. Have faith in yourself," I said. "Watch me, and I'll come back if you need me to."

I leaped to the balcony then motioned for her to follow. I glanced in the window. Richard was still sleeping, mostly induced by his own exhaustion.

She crouched then jumped hard, surpassing the ledge, but instead of panicking, she maintained self-control and gracefully glided back, landing quietly beside me.

"Make sure to shut the blind so the hole in the window will not be discovered until you are gone. Will you be all right?"

"I am now," she said, and she kissed me tenderly.

I hugged her hard, not wanting to let go, but there was no other choice.

"No matter what, stay linked with me. You need to quietly reconnect yourself to the medical equipment. It must not look like anything has been tampered with. Let me know when you are ready." She nodded and squeezed my hand one more time before letting go. I watched her slip through the cut glass, and then I jumped down from the ledge and stood in the alley below. I was not worried about the light. I had my dark sunglasses. I began to listen and focus on her. I thought of the first time I met her and of how blindingly white her aura was. Her light filled the dark, empty places of my soul.

Thad, I'm ready, she called to me.

I quickly flooded her mind with our many walks together through the forest near her home, of how I saw her glowing beauty in the moonlight, and of the night I gave her the necklace. I gave her as many of my treasured thoughts as I could muster. Then I put her under my spell.

Sleep, Rhymee. Still your breath, your blood, and your heart. Do not wake until you hear my voice.

When the heart monitor's alarm pierced my ears, I knew my spell had worked and that Rhymee would appear dead until I called to her. I wanted to stay near her, but I needed to take care of something alone, and I could not put the task off.

MEETING MR. JENKINS

It was like I was in a comatose state when I heard my father panicking. I didn't feel the need to move, and I wasn't sad. His voice was like a pinprick that couldn't break into my blissful world. Seeing visions through Thadacus was real, and my dad was the dream.

I heard my dad leap from his chair. I felt him grasp my left hand. He couldn't click the button that called the nurse's station enough.

"Rhymee, please stay with us," he begged. I felt his tears falling on my face.

I heard a nurse rush in. "Mr. Stewart, please move so that I can try and help her."

Moments later, other attendants hurried in and began trying to revive me. My dad was asked to leave the room. Once he reached the hall, he began sobbing louder and louder.

It sort of felt like bothersome flies landing on my skin as the doctors and nurses prodded and poked on me. This went on for a short while, and then my hospital room was quiet.

I was not aware of how much time had passed when I again heard my dad speaking in some far off distance.

"I just got off the phone with my wife. She is on her way here. What do we need to do to take Rhymee from here?"

"I will have the physician get the paperwork in order. I suggest you call the local funeral home. They can help you with the funeral arrangements."

"Thank you for helping," Dad said.

"I am sorry you are going through this, Mr. Stewart. I will be back in a moment," said the nurse, exiting the room.

Soon, my mom arrived. She hugged my dad tightly. "I'm sorry I wasn't here, Richard."

"Bhren, why did this happen to her of all people? I should've made her go with us too that day. It's my fault she's dead."

"It's just as much mine, Richard."

I could hear them both weeping.

"Have you told Rhondel and Rhegan?"

"I couldn't bear to. I was trying so hard not to cry as I left them with Hada. They knew something was wrong, and I think they suspect, but you and I both need to be there when we tell them. Don't you agree?"

"Yes," Dad choked.

After my parents left, I soon heard two men pull a squeaky stretcher into the room. I felt like I was floating as they transferred me from the bed to the harder surface. Then a blanket grazed my face as they covered me. As I was wheeled to the elevator, I caught many scents: alcohol, peroxide, stored liquid and powder drugs, and cleaning agents mixing with and covering the smell of sickness, but it all seemed of little consequence. I didn't want to be bothered while I was with Thad.

I heard an engine start as I was loaded into a stale-smelling vehicle. The driver of the vehicle unwrapped a brown paper bag, opened a bag of chips and a can of pop, and began eating a bacon, lettuce, and tomato sandwich as we pulled out of the parking lot

He drove for several miles before stopping. He chugged the last of his drink and belched loudly. He quickly rolled the window down and sighed. He sat there for a few more minutes before deciding to get out and go inside.

It was quiet for a long while, and I enjoyed the silence of the outside world. Thad's sultry voice was the only one that I wanted to hear. *I will protect you forever, Rhymee,* he whispered, holding me tightly.

We were again disturbed when the double doors of the vehicle were flung open.

"Where do you want her, Harold?" the driver asked.

Two other men and a woman had also gathered around the vehicle.

"Her parents want her cremated. Take her to the crematorium."

"They don't want to hold a viewing?" asked the woman.

"No, Mr. Stewart explained that it was too painful for the family. They are holding a private service for her at their house. Now, please get her moved. I have other matters to attend to."

The men huffed as they pulled the gurney from the van. The woman just stood there and watched. Once we were moving, she struggled to keep up in her high heels. Numerous doors opened and closed until we entered a stifling hot room. I could smell rotting flesh, bone, and ash. I could hear a roaring industrial furnace not far from where I was. *Thad, I want to leave this place. Where have you taken me?*

Rhymee, when you no longer hear anyone, wake up, but do not move unless you feel threatened. When you wake, you will know where you are. I will come for you as quickly as possible. I am leaving the farm now.

Everyone left the room, except one man and the woman. She walked over and grabbed a clipboard hanging from the wall. A pen resting inside the clip fell to the floor.

"Could this day be any more tiring?" she said, bending to pick it back up.

"Where do you want her, Joan?" the man asked.

"Over there with those two. I'll get to the three of them tomorrow."

"May I take a peek?" he asked, after pushing me to a corner. I was thankful he had moved me. I was farther from the heat.

"I suppose, but make it quick. I've had a long day, and I'm sick of Harold breathing down my throat."

The man lifted the sheet covering my face and gasped. "She's so young...and breathtaking. What happened to her?"

I could feel him staring at me.

Joan whirled around. "She was stabbed to death. Now cover her back up, Greg."

Greg stared at me for a moment longer, and then he did as he was told. "Are we still on for Friday night, dinner and a movie?"

"Yes, call me later. Now, I need to go meet with Jenkins. We have a family arriving at four o'clock to look at caskets."

When the two of them finally left, I woke. I remembered everything: my parents' reactions to my death, my torturous ride in the back of a smelly van, arriving at this torturous inferno, and finally, I remembered my overwhelming grief. I wanted to run to my family and reassure them that I was okay, but I knew I couldn't. They would not understand my sudden transformation. It would terrify them. I had kept Thad a secret, and it was too late to fess up to them now.

Thad, hurry. I don't like where I'm at.

I am on my way, Rhymee. I will be there within minutes, but do not come to me until I call to you.

Okay.

I sighed then pulled the thick sheet from my face and turned my head sideways. I was lying beside two other dead bodies, but they were also covered with sheets. Unlike the man, Greg, I didn't want to look at them. I could smell the noxious gases building within them from bacteria feeding on their decaying flesh. Their bodies were already beginning to bloat. I gagged at the thought.

I heard someone enter the funeral home's reception area.

"May I help you, Sir?" I heard Joan ask. "Did you have an appointment? We are going to close soon."

"Yes, I would like to speak to the funeral director, Harold Jenkins," requested Thad.

When I heard his voice, my heart skipped a beat, and my sadness was stifled for the moment.

"I'm sorry. He's unavailable. He's in a meeting."

"I will wait. Will you let him know I am the cousin of the young girl that was brought in today? Her parents did not want to hold a viewing, but I was very close to my cousin. I would like to pay my final respects before she is cremated."

I could feel the hint of a strange desire stir within Thad, but I could tell he was suppressing it and shielding most of it from me. Was it his hunger? I was too distraught to ask questions. I just wanted to leave this awful place.

"Please take a seat," requested Joan.

Rhymee, it will not be much longer.

I know. I'm all right.

It was after five o'clock when Harold Jenkins agreed to see Thad. Thad and I both laughed to each other when Joan told Mr. Jenkins that she didn't like the looks of the man in the reception area.

"Will that be all for the day, Mr. Jenkins?" asked Joan as they both stepped out of his office.

"Yes, thank you, Joan," said Mr. Jenkins, walking toward Thad. "I am sorry, who are you again?"

"My name is John. I chuckled when Thad didn't use his real name. "I would like to see my cousin one last time while she is still intact."

"Well, this is highly unusual. I will need to call her family."

I could hear Thad reach in his pocket and pull out a wad of cash. "Is that really necessary?"

Mr. Jenkins swallowed deeply. "You'll need to make it quick."

"Of course," said Thad, handing him the cash.

"Follow me."

I could hear the two of them coming, and I knew there was no one else in the building besides the three of us. *What should I do, Thad?*

Cover up. Do not move until I tell you to.

K. I quickly pulled the sheet over my head and closed my eyes. I could hear them walking down the long hallway. Shortly afterward, I heard the doors to the room I was in swing open.

Once inside, Jenkins stopped and looked around for a moment. "Ah, there she is."

He walked over to where I was, but pulled the sheet back from the elderly dead man lying beside me. "Oh, wrong one. You can never tell when they're covered. You're lucky; Joan was going to process the three of them today but ran out of time."

He then pulled the sheet from my face. I could feel his eyes fixate on me.

"She looks so peaceful."

"That line of bull makes me sick. I have heard it for centuries. Is that your way of making small talk, Jenkins? Death robs people from all the pleasures in life. They are only peaceful because they know nothing and feel nothing," said Thad somewhat sarcastically.

But before Mr. Jenkins could say anything, Thad dashed to the door, locked it, and turned out the lights.

"What's the meaning of this? Why did you turn the lights out? I can't see anything?"

"Do not move," Thad demanded, removing his sunglasses.

"What are you?" asked Jenkins, staring at his glowing eyes.

"I am a vampire, and so is she. Rhymee, show him."

"Hello," I said, sitting up. Mr. Jenkins was long limbed, with a very pronounced chin and forehead. He was shaped like an upside-down triangle, reminding me of a rosy-cheeked goon. For some strange reason, I couldn't help exposing my fangs and flashing my glimmering green eyes. Looking at the funeral director sent chills down my spine. I was suddenly excited, but why?

First, Mr. Jenkins tripped over the chair and fumbled to the ground, and then he slowly stood up and backed himself in a corner. "By the looks of you, I knew you were untrustworthy."

"It is regrettable that you must keep a hard secret," Thad began.

"What are you talking about?"

"We will not hurt you—that is, if you listen and follow our instruction. Understood?" asked Thad.

"What do you want?" weakly asked Jenkins.

"You will produce an urn full of ash. I don't care what's in the urn as long as it looks authentic. Use one of those bodies if you must," Thad glanced at the two corpses near me. "You can tell Joan you worked through the night to help her catch up. When Rhymee's family comes to pick up her remains, you are to act normal and hand them the fake urn. You are to never speak of us to anyone. Am I clear?"

"Are you going to kill me after that?"

"You are safe unless you expose us. Know that our powers are limitless, and we are invulnerable. I will know if you so much as whisper our names. I will not kill you quickly. You will be tortured. I consider myself good hearted, but cross me on this matter, and you shall see the dark side of my nature," warned Thad.

"Your secret is safe, and I will make the preparations," said Jenkins shakily. Then he turned to me. "I am sorry this happened to you, child."

When he said that, I was reminded of my family and the pain they were going through. "Thad, may we go now?" I jumped off the gurney.

"I need to do one more thing, Rhymee…. Jenkins, is there a needle around here somewhere?"

"Over there," he pointed.

"Good, go prick your finger with it then."

"What?"

"You heard me. I need to swallow a small drop of your blood."

My eyes widened. *What?*

It's okay, Rhymee. I am not going to hurt him. I will explain later.

"Why?" asked Mr. Jenkins.

"Insurance. After I swallow a drop of your blood, I will know your every thought if I choose to listen. You best not betray us."

Mr. Jenkins began to breathe heavily. "Your secret is safe. I swear on my life I won't tell a soul about the two of you." His heart raced even faster. "Please don't kill me." He was terrified.

"I will admit I have thought about it. The light emanating from around your body tells me a few things about your character. I have seen that shade of purple more times than I care to remember. You're a liar, Mr. Jenkins, and you steal from people often. I do not trust your word. I suggest you change your ways before it is too late. However, I will not kill you. Now, get on with it. Prick your finger. Rhymee has been in this vile place long enough."

Mr. Jenkin's heart slowed a little as he walked over to a shelf that held numerous, odd tools and picked up a large hypodermic needle. "You know, I have no reason to trust you either. Just look at what you have done to this innocent girl," he sighed, poking his finger. A small drop of blood oozed to the surface of his skin. The blood radiated like a rich orange fire.

When he accused Thad, my anger rose. "You've no idea what he's done for me, and it's none of your business." My throat felt icy. My body was chilled. I began to shiver uncontrollably. I was drawn to the blood. I knew it would warm me. I didn't shield my desire from Thad. I wanted him to know how I felt so that he could help me.

When he looked at me, he seemed slightly alarmed. *Rhymee, wait outside the door. I will be right there.*

I trusted Thad with my life, so I quickly did as he said.

While standing in the hall, I heard Mr. Jenkins shudder when Thad licked his finger. "Now, please leave."

"Gladly."

Thad stormed through the doors and grabbed my hand. "Let's get out of here."

I stopped for a second outside and took a breath of fresh air.

"Are you okay, Rhymee? I am sorry you had to go through all of that."

I nodded. "I felt warmer when I entered the hall. Did you mean it, Thad? Would you really kill Mr. Jenkins?"

"If he betrays us, he will die. Rhymee, it would be best if you left this area for a long while."

"Where would we go? I don't know that I am ready to leave my family. Couldn't I watch them from a distance?"

"If you are seen by anyone who recognizes you, it could be bad."

"Oh."

"I could show you where I hail from and the places I have stayed. We can visit my friends Savora and Michael."

"Thad, I know you're right, but the thoughts of leaving my mom, my dad…my sisters….It's breaking my heart."

"Rhymee, I wish I could change things. It is my fault you are in pain. I wish you were a normal teenager again." I could feel a mixture of sadness and anger rise within him, and I knew he was mad at himself.

I hugged him, opening my thoughts to him. I wanted him to feel how much I loved him. "I want to go with you. I just need a couple days to say my good-byes in my own way. I promise they won't know I'm there."

Thad squeezed me tightly.

"Where do we go now?"

"Can you handle returning to the farm? Hopefully, everyone will be asleep. I need to take care of some unfinished business. We will be gone by daybreak, but we will return so that you may see them before we leave for good."

"Will I ever get to see them after that?"

"We may return from time to time, but they must not know you exist."

I sighed and nodded. "What unfinished business?"

I had a suspicion of what he was up to, but I didn't say anything. I too wanted to know where the crazy woman that tried to kill me had gone.

THE HUNT

While Rhymee was being transported from the hospital to the crematory, I hurried back to the farm. I wanted to know more about Rhymee's attacker. I wanted a clear picture of where she had gone and what she had done once she fled. I followed the faded, stale path of blood until I reached the highway. A pool of it, no longer visible to a human's naked eye, saturated the soil. I dreaded what I did next. I scooped a large clump of the caked, blood-dirt mixture and put it in my mouth. My saliva began to slowly dissolve it. Hazel's blood was like a tattletale. I could suddenly feel the pain in her arm as the wet grit fought its way down my throat. I closed my eyes and focused on the night Rhymee was attacked. I saw everything. I immediately knew Hazel Mirerott and her memories. Just like my other victims, I would have a mental connection with her until the day of her death.

Hazel stood for a moment in shock. Her arm had been mutilated by birdshot.

"Foolish girl!" she shouted in pain. "This wound is nothing compared to the one I'm about to inflict upon you! Lurhide is not going to like it that I've been injured! I must finish the job, or there will be no eternity for me," she wailed, still intent on killing.

Rhymee lay unconscious on the floor next to the gun.

Headlights began to glow from outside. Rhymee's parents were back early.

"Great! What else could go wrong?" muttered Hazel, darting out the kitchen door. She scuffled through the woods, tripping now and again on roots and undergrowth, but she didn't slow, not even for the throbbing in her wounded arm. She could feel blood soaking through her sleeve and down her waist. She knew she was leaving a trail, but she had no time to cover her tracks. She would hitch a ride once she reached the main highway.

Suddenly she was stopped by a red mist zigzagging along the ground.

"This is not good! Salumus wanted you alive so you could help destroy the others! You have left a trail of blood! Can you not follow simple instructions?" barked the mercuride I had overheard in the cavern called Lurhide.

"I'm alive, aren't I?"

"Not for long! The vampire will have his day with you!"

"If he can find me!"

"Hazel, I fear for you, and you are one of our best. How did she injure you?"

"The girl knew I was coming! How, I don't know. She had a gun!"

"I warned you. The girl is cunning," said Lurhide.

"Not for long. She will die! I got her. It's just a matter of time," explained Hazel, her tongue writhing with gratification. "Tell me, Master, will Salumus still grant me immortality since I succeeded in causing her death?"

"That depends on if you live long enough to complete your mission. The girl is not the only one he needed your help with," answered Lurhide. "If you die before it is time, he will not be pleased."

"This is nothing. I will tend to it once I reach a room," reassured Hazel, holding up her arm.

"It's not the arm I'm worried about!"

Lights flashed, and sirens sounded in the distance. Hazel didn't take heed until she heard dogs barking.

"I best move lest I get caught."

"Go on! I will know where to find you, if I have need!" ordered Lurhide.

It wasn't long before Hazel reached the main road. She took the scarf from around her hair and used it to wave at oncoming traffic while hiding her damaged, crimson-stained side.

Soon a trucker slammed on his breaks.

At first, she aimed to kill the driver but then thought it might not be a good idea in case there was a roadblock somewhere.

"Need a ride, ma'am?" asked the man after sliding over and opening his passenger side door.

What an idiot! Of course I do, thought Hazel as she smiled.

"Yes, please. You see, my boyfriend left me out here. We had a fight, and he hit me pretty hard with his lug wrench," she lied in her most desperate voice, deciding to show her bloody arm.

"What a creep! I will get you to a hospital. Are you able to climb up in here?" he asked, patting the seat.

Hazel was alarmed by his offer to take her to the hospital, but she kept her cool. "Yes! Thank you so much! You are a lifesaver!"

"You will have to guide me. I am not from around here. I'm afraid I don't know where the nearest hospital is. By the way, my name is Ron. What's yours, if I may ask?"

"Hazel," she replied, delighting in the fact the driver was not familiar with the area. She would direct him to the interstate and then kill him once clear of all possible roadblocks.

I later discovered that Hazel had succeeded in her plan, and Ron was lying in a ditch along the highway dead. Hazel drove the trucker's semi until she passed a cheap motel called the Free Spirit, but instead of stopping, she drove by and parked the semi at a gas station a couple miles down the road.

She grabbed a first aid kit, some of Ron's clothes, which were a little big but would have to do, and his cigarettes. She packed them in a nylon duffle bag then began to walk cautiously back to the motel. She scoped out a vacant room, quickly and effortlessly picked the lock on number thirty-four, and entered.

"Hmm, I guess this will have to do," she said to herself, noticing how shabby the place was.

After closing the curtains, she took a hot shower and began picking the birdshot from her wounded arm with the tweezers she had found inside the kit. When she was finished, she poured peroxide over the entire area, let it froth violently for a moment, and then she repeated the step. After she wrapped the wound in gauze and secured it with white hospital tape, she crashed on the bed and had a cigarette. She set her watch for 4:00 a.m.

Rhymee followed me to the edge of the woods. She looked troubled.

"Thadacus, I feel awkward, unlike last night," she said, grabbing my hands.

"It will be okay. It is because you need to feed. You will have to hunt as I do," I explained, feeling a little apprehensive because she had never killed.

She looked out into the night, sniffed the air, and then seemed to read my facial expressions.

"Don't worry, Thad. I can hunt. As a matter of fact, I will lead the way. I just follow my nose, right?" she asked, seeming to pick up a scent I had already detected.

"Well, if you know who it is you are hunting, but sometimes you must watch for the corrupt and follow them to make sure they are not innocent. But make no mistake. It is never easy to act as judge and punisher. Anger toward their vile crimes must consume me, or they might try to harm me before I can act, and I still must live with my conscience," I said, trying to prepare her.

"Since the first time I found out what you were and how you hunted, I've asked myself if I could do the same. I wouldn't have let you turn me, Thadacus, if I thought I could not have handled this part." She gently kissed me.

I closed my eyes and savored the moment.

"I'm hungry," she said in a gentle, needy voice.

"Whose scent do you detect?" I asked.

"It belongs to the crazy woman who stabbed me," said Rhymee.

"How do you know it is not animal blood?" I asked, already aware that the outdated odor was that of a human's.

"She had a smell all right, only hers was not pleasant. Her armpits were the worst. I don't think she had bathed in at least a week. Her sweat is mixed with the blood. My first instinct was not to trust her, but she put on a good act, and I thought I was being inhospitable."

"Show me the scent, and I shall help," I said, wanting to teach Rhymee, but there was one thing I was quite certain of: this hunt would be a successful one. I would make sure of it.

Rhymee did not have to step far. She bent down, picked up a leaf, held it to her nose, and inhaled deeply.

"This has her scent," she said, handing me the leaf.

I studied it for a moment and noticed it held a spot of dried blood.

"I have got it, but I shall let you lead the way," I said, urging her to use her instincts.

She gave me a devious smile and began tracking. We cut right through the center of the forest. Rhymee would stop every once in a while and just stare.

"What is it? Did you find a trace of her?" I asked, knowing we were on the right path.

"No, it's just that…see that moth?" asked Rhymee, pointing to the bark of a tree where it rested.

"Yes," I softly answered.

"I wouldn't have seen it as a human. I didn't realize how blind I was, Thadacus, even in the light of day," she said, amazed. She turned her attention to the sky. "It hurts to look at the moon and stars almost as much as it once did looking directly into the sun."

"I was amazed in much the same way the first time I viewed the world with these magical eyes. Although it was different for me. I have very few memories of my humanity."

"Why, Thad?" asked Rhymee, concerned. "I can remember everything."

"I do not fully understand. I will tell you what I know later on when we have more time. It is a long story."

"We've not talked in a long while. I look forward to that later," she said, stepping forward a few feet.

"Me too."

She knelt down to a tree root that was protruding from the ground in scattered spots and examined the area.

"She tripped over this root," said Rhymee, sounding certain of her deduction.

"What tells you that?"

"See how there is more than just a drop of dried blood staining the ground in that depression?"

"Yes," I answered.

"She fell and landed there on her injured arm. It looks like she hit the ground a few times out of frustration and anger, struggled to get up, and then headed in that direction." Rhymee pointed. "My dad taught me how to track."

"Your instincts are quite keen," I commended. I felt her become slightly upset again at the thought of her dad.

Shortly thereafter, we climbed a ravine and were standing at a section of the fog-covered highway. Rhymee sniffed the air and ground.

"Her scent has faded." She became discouraged.

"From here it will be harder to follow her because the witch covers her tracks," I said, craving revenge. "Would you like me to take the lead?"

"Can you tell me if I am right?" asked Rhymee.

"Only if you will kiss me afterward." I beamed.

"Deal." She laughed.

"West?" she asked, moving closer to me. "Am I correct?"

"You are," I answered, gently kissing her cheek.

Excited, she began to sprint. I followed. We did not stop until we had crossed into Oklahoma.

"Thad, am I crazy, or is her scent mixed in with someone else's?"

Every once in a while, a cigarette had been flung out the window, and it was not Hazel's.

"She rides with someone, a male," I said. "He feeds on—"

"Pork rinds," interjected Rhymee. "Disgusting."

Twenty miles from that point, we discovered the spot where the man had been dumped, and we knew he had been either badly injured or murdered.

"He was probably trying to help her like I was," she said, feeling sorry for the guy.

"Rhymee, we need to find somewhere to shelter soon. Daylight approaches," I mentioned, resting my hand on her shoulder.

We continued to track, but at the same time we searched for a place to spend the day.

"Her odor is suddenly strong. It's coming from there," she said, pointing in the direction of a poorly maintained motel. "The Free Spirit, hmm…I suppose we can stay there. Maybe we can find some clues."

"Umm, how about no. I will not have my lady staying in such a place. I have a better idea," I said, seeing a sign for a ritzy hotel called the Grant Monroe. "We will make a stop here after dark."

"A coldness is growing inside me. I'm hungry, Thad," said Rhymee, sounding miserable.

"Come on. I will help take your mind off things."

"Oh really! What do you have in mind?"

"Nothing too bad." I laughed. "I do remember I was once an honorable man."

Rhymee put her head down shyly.

"Follow me," I said, chuckling. We darted a few miles down the road, and then I casually walked into the hotel and got us a room. While Rhymee was in the shower, I went down the street to the twenty-four-hour supercenter and bought us each a set of new clothes, and although we did not need to sleep, I bought myself a pair of boxers and for Rhymee I bought a new set of cotton pajamas, a cheap backpack, and a pair of dark sunglasses. The clothes were not name brand as I liked, but they would have to do.

I made it back to the room right as the sun began to rise. I quickly closed the curtains and laid Rhymee's new items neatly on her bed. I then turned on the television, sat at the edge of my bed, and listened to the news.

"The body of a forty-year-old, Ron Harding, was identified by family early this morning. Investigators are still trying to find Harding's murderer. When we return, we'll take a look at your local weather. This is Carrie Smith with CFV News," said the reporter, giving a fake smile right before the commercials hit.

Rhymee exited the bathroom, tightly wrapped in a white towel. Her green eyes were like flares piercing through the steam that encompassed her after her extremely hot shower. Strands of her wet auburn hair stuck to her forehead and cheeks, amplifying her expression of wild hunger. She was stunning. I couldn't take my eyes off her.

"Your turn," she said, unaware of the affect she had on me.

"I got you some new things," I said, pointing to the bed. "I will try to hurry."

The hot, pounding water from this hotel's showerhead would have made a human's skin appear sunburned, but my olive complexion remained unscathed. The heat was only soothing, and if it had been boiling, it would have had the same effect. My nerve endings simply no longer warned me of bodily damage by causing pain, unless something deeply penetrated my skin.

I closed my eyes as the water flowed over my hair. There really was no need to wash with soap; a vampire's glands do not secrete human odors. However, it is necessary to rinse away the dirt and sometimes dried blood after traveling through dense forest or after a gruesome kill.

I was startled. Glass crashed and shattered against the wall. It took seconds to thrust my jeans onto my wet body as I raced to Rhymee. I was instantly in a kill-and-protect mode.

I didn't see her, and then she gasped. I found her hunched over on her knees on the other side of her bed.

I ran and grabbed her.

"Rhymee, what happened?" I asked panicked.

"I took…a…sip…"

She pointed to the broken glass and wet carpet. She had tried to drink water.

I sat down on the floor next to her and then cradled her between my legs.

"I can help. Let me rub your stomach," I said gently. "Rest your head and shut your eyes."

"I was…so…hungry. I thought…"

"Shh, I understand. I have done the same thing. It is my fault. I forgot to tell you that to drink water would cause pain," I explained while kneading her stomach like dough. "Is it getting any better?"

"A little. Thanks. Why does water do that?" she asked, relaxing just a little.

"It accelerates your hunger beyond ravenous, especially if you have not eaten, and supplies no sustenance. It should not last much longer."

Her breathing slowed.

"You once drank water by accident?" she asked, assuming I had consumed it unintentionally.

"I once drank deliberately to remind myself of what pain felt like," I admitted, now somewhat ashamed of that decision.

"Thad, I'm sorry. I threw the glass out of anger. I can't control it when I'm in such pain," she admitted, halfway expecting me to be mad at her.

"I understand," I said softly.

Knock! Knock! Knock!

"Stay still. I will take care of this," I said, carefully laying her flat on the floor.

I grabbed my shades from the dresser then opened the door.

"Can I do something for you?" I asked the young man from room service.

"The adjoining room complained of a noise, sir. I was told to check on it," he said, trying to see around my body into the room.

"I accidentally broke a glass. I tripped and knocked it off the bar. I am quite clumsy, you know," I said. "Please apologize to the people next door for me."

"I will send someone up to have the glass cleaned," he said, still trying to see inside, which irritated me.

"Not until after we check out. I don't wish to be disturbed this morning. Now, if you will kindly excuse me," I said curtly.

"Oh, of course, sir! Sorry to have disturbed you."

I quickly pulled the covers back on Rhymee's bed, fluffed her pillow, lifted her from the floor, and then tucked her in the bed.

She hugged me tightly for a moment then gave me a deep look.

"I could squeeze you to death. I want to be that close to you," she said lovingly.

"You can try, if you like," I answered, daring her.

She smiled while biting at her nails. She was slightly frustrated when the tips remained intact rather than chunks shredding away as before.

Although she seemed to be over the effects of the water, I could tell hunger was seething inside her, and she was agitated.

"Come here then," she requested with a passionate voice.

I pounced on her bed and cradled her in my arms until I could see darkness slowly emerge and spread from under the heavy hotel drapes like spilled ink.

When we were ready to continue tracking, I severed my mind from Rhymee's. She packed our few belongings as I wiped everything down and bagged the broken glass. "Thad, why are we cleaning like this? Won't room service take care of it?"

"Rhymee, we don't exist. It is best that we do not leave any indications behind that we were here."

We took the elevator down to the main floor and left the hotel through the side doors. "Try and pick up her scent as I chunk this."

Rhymee nodded and concentrated on the breeze. "We should return to that motel, The Free Spirit."

As I walked over to the dumpster and threw the glass in, I again focused on Hazel. "Good idea."

When we reached The Free Spirit, we stood at a distance, watching and listening. There were only a few vehicles parked out front, and I could only hear three people moving around and talking inside. At the moment, the motel had numerous vacancies. The navy-blue paint on the outside walls, the cedar-trimmed window seals, and the parking lot were all warped and cracked with age. We cautiously walked around to where Hazel's room was located, which was not visible from the main office, and approached the door.

Even though it was locked, I twisted the knob with ease and gained access to the musty room. The scuffed furniture, macramé lamp shades, and burnt-orange shag carpet were from the seventies.

"I would prefer sleeping in a damp cave rather than this," I said, noticing a few holes punched through the brown paneling.

"I hear things crawling inside the mattress."

"Don't go near it. It's bed bugs."

"Eww, gross," whispered Rhymee, grabbing my arm.

"We will not be here long."

"Good."

The floor had been vacuumed since Hazel's stay but not cleaned with water. Her blood had dribbled in small spots, leading to the bathroom. I walked over and knelt down to the largest drop and scrapped flakes of it from the matted carpet fibers.

"What's that for?" asked Rhymee.

I sprinkled the flakes on my tongue, and within seconds, images of what Hazel had recently been doing flashed before me. "Do you want to try it, Rhymee? You will be able to see what she has been up since we started tracking her."

"Uh, no thanks," she quietly chuckled. "And you are so brushing your teeth before I kiss you."

I laughed, closed my eyes, and focused.

More of Hazel's memories flashed through my mind. The first one was of her getting into bed at the motel.

"The vampire won't track me now. I smell like that filthy trucker," the crone muttered to herself, right before drifting to sleep.

I also saw that before the police discovered the abandoned semi and Ron's body, Hazel had hitchhiked completely across the panhandle of Oklahoma and entered New Mexico. From there, she intended to turn south. At first she didn't know where she was headed, but she finally decided Albuquerque would be a good hiding place. She had visited the city before so had an idea of where she could establish herself for a while.

Then I witnessed Hazel stepping in a pile of human waste, almost causing her to trip as she crossed the dark hall to the staircase of the zoo house she was staying in. It was a place where drug addicts not only could purchase drugs but also a lawless place where they could stay while using them. A half-dressed crackhead was out cold a few feet from his accident. His track-marked arm, which still held a half-full hypodermic needle, was stretched out, seeming to call for a helping hand.

She ran over, grabbed the needle, and finished the injection.

"There. Maybe that will kill you, you gross piece of filth," she said calmly. Then she ascended the stairs.

Through Hazel's eyes, I saw a tall, dark man wearing a dingy white t-shirt and a pair of black leather pants standing from the balcony.

"Oh! Anton! I didn't see you there," said Hazel, surprised.

"I know," Anton replied angrily, twisting the gold ring on his index finger nervously.

"I'm sorry, Anton," replied Hazel humbly. "I know you've done me a favor by letting me stay here."

"You're dang straight, so don't go to killing my customers!"

"I know. I just have a hatred for them. I won't do it again. I shouldn't have to stay here much longer."

"Do you have my cut?" he asked.

I experienced a sudden flashback with Hazel. I felt her trepidation of bringing all her cash into that place; thieves lurked around every corner. She had opened a safety deposit box two years earlier in this city and had stashed away several thousand dollars from her last job. She was a miser and was used to living in terrible conditions. She didn't want to change because she knew her personality wouldn't fit in any other level of society.

She reached down deep in her pocket and pulled out a wad of cash.

"It's all I have," she lied, handing him three hundred dollars.

"You're breaking me." He shook his head, indicating he wasn't happy.

"It'll have to do," she responded in a somewhat threatening tone. "Now, if you'll excuse me, I need to get to my room."

"I ought to beat you bloody, but I could see you stabbing me in my sleep or something. Besides, I need your rent money," said the man.

"Why, Anton, you have come to know me so well," she said, continuing toward the stairwell.

Upon reaching her room, Hazel sat down on the thin, striped mattress, which was saturated with urine and bloodstains.

"Thank goodness I have a new high-priced target. I don't know how much more I can stomach this place," she said.

She stood up and was changing clothes when suddenly she had an unexpected visitor.

"Hazzzelll, geettt dresssed," informed Lurhide with a distorted voice, still trying to take shape in the corner of the room.

"What's wrong?" responded Hazel, making haste. "Why?"

"Although Salumus is not pleased with your work as of late, he wanted me to warn you," said the mercuride, soon perched in her normal majestic stance, wings outstretched. "You are lucky he is so forgiving."

"Warn me of what?"

"You failed with the girl, and she now hunts you."

"I will kill her this time," said Hazel, glancing at her knives.

"You are powerless against her!" explained Lurhide scornfully. "Since you fell short of your task, she is now vampire, the most powerful one in existence, and she does not pursue you alone. The male is with her, helping. His vengeance is relentless. I myself think you shall meet a horrible end, Hazel Mirerott, and there is nothing I can do to save you."

"I covered my tracks and scent well. They will not find me," she said with confidence.

"They are just miles away. You foolishly underestimate their abilities."

"Death does not scare me, but I was promised immortality!" Hazel trembled, nearly throwing a fit. "I feel I have been cheated, and Salumus is full of empty promises."

"How dare you speak of him in such a way! I shall let him know how you feel!" snapped Lurhide. "I should not have come here to warn you. You deserve to die, you repulsive, ungrateful human!"

"Huh!" Hazel stomped. "Go ahead! I now realize I made a grave mistake getting mixed up with the lot of you!"

The mercuride left without saying another word.

Hazel grabbed her purse and darted down the stairs.

"Where are you going at this hour?" asked Anton, blocking Hazel at the front door.

"Out of my way, less you wish to die!" snarled Hazel.

"Okay, but you don't have to be such a witch!" said Anton, letting her go. "Chill out!"

"If you knew what was coming for me, you would hide!"

"Did you lead the cops here?" asked Anton, enraged.

"It's much worse! You wouldn't believe me even if I told you, and there's no time to explain. Now move!"

"Fine," said Anton, moving his arm.

Hazel stepped out the door then suddenly turned.

"By the way, give me the cash back. I won't be renting from you this week," she ordered, wrenching her fingers back and forth.

By the dire look on Hazel's face, Anton knew she spoke the truth. He sighed and then handed her the money.

She didn't walk, she ran to the nearest bus station, paid the fair on Amerimap's bus number 8, heading to Sacramento, California. She didn't care where the bus was headed as long as she was on the move.

We did not linger long at the motel. Rhymee was so hungry that once she picked up on the trail, she began to run hard.

"Thad, how long can a vampire go without eating?" she turned and asked, seeming a little crazed.

"You would be surprised," I replied. "You are in no danger of starvation, although you may feel like it."

Rhymee stopped for a moment to listen.

"It would take longer than a year to starve to death."

"I feel like it's happening right now." Rhymee gasped, grabbing her stomach.

"It will never be this bad again. The gnawing hunger is always at its worst when one is first turned."

Tracks created from a special concoction of residual drugs, human decay, and Hazel's heavy perfume stained the streets and sidewalks for miles away from the yellow, paint-cracked place of self-inflicted human suffering known as the zoo house. In my opinion, it was a rat's den.

"I've lost my appetite," said Rhymee in disgust, cautiously entering the poorly lit foyer behind me.

A woman, with eyes occasionally rolling to the back of her head, was leaned against a wall.

"Can I...I...I help you?" she asked, beginning to stagger toward us in a pair of open-toed stilettos.

I looked around and sniffed the air, halfway ignoring her.

Rhymee grabbed my arm, insecure about the whole situation.

"Are you okay?" I asked her.

She slowly nodded yes, still in shock people behaved like that. "It's just that I—"

The delusional woman suddenly reached for Rhymee's arm. "Got any money, girly?" she asked with an unnatural, wide smile. I grabbed her wrist. I wanted to break it, but I restrained myself in front of Rhymee. I knew any more pressure from my squeeze would have shattered the woman's bones.

"I peed myself." She laughed. "Your touch is a ride, man. What are you on?"

I threw her arm harshly, letting her go. "Back off," I threatened with exposed fangs.

"You got any money for Joanna?" she asked, ignoring my warnings.

My patience had run out. I lifted her up and tossed her across the room, knocking her cold.

I was growing hungry, but I did not want to feed on a drug addict. The drugs would not have had any effect on me, but I did not want the substances in my body. I viewed the addicts as stupid, not evil.

We flung every door open upstairs and down, finding rooms full of strung-out drug heads, but there was no sign of our prey. We did, however, manage to find one drug-free miscreant hiding in a small closet under the staircase.

"Who are you?" I asked, pulling him out by the nape of his neck.

"Puh…ple…please don't hurt me," he begged, shaking all over. "I am Anton Seneca."

Like that name meant anything to me. He was worse than the vermin he supplied drugs to. "We are searching for a woman," I said forcibly.

"I…I have plenty of those here. What kind of woman?" he asked in a shaky, yet business voice.

"A crazy, drug-free one," I answered.

"Oh," he responded, sounding disappointed, knowing he had no woman like that.

"Rhymee, go ahead and describe her to him," I softly requested.

"She is blonde, about five six, has a pointy nose, and looks to be in her early forties. She would have had an injured arm," she explained, trying to sound tough.

I cracked a small smile.

"Hazel!" the man blurted. "Trust me. You don't want to find her. She's a killer."

"Where is she?" asked Rhymee impatiently.

"She left earlier this evening."

"Where was she headed?" I asked.

"Don't know. She left in a hurry, said something about being in danger. Look, man. She was just a renter. I've known her for a long time, but she comes and goes as she pleases. I don't keep up with her or her business."

"Right," said Rhymee, calling him a liar in a roundabout way.

I slowly let go of him. "We are finished here," I told Rhymee.

She turned and walked toward the front door, and I followed.

However, Anton was not finished, the stupid fool. He pulled a small pistol from his pocket and shot me in the back.

I snarled out of pain and anger. "Rhymee, wait for me outside!" I gasped.

"Thad!" she screamed.

"I'm okay! I don't want you to watch me feed!"

She stood there with a reluctant, frightened look, torn between doing as I requested and coming to my aid.

Click!

I again heard the trigger pull back on Anton's pistol. I turned to see his trembling hand take aim. He intended to kill me.

"Why aren't you dead?" he yelled in disbelief.

"Rhymee, go!" I ordered.

That time she listened and left. She waited outside till I was finished. I did not share my kill for two reasons. I knew Rhymee needed to stay hungry so she would continue to hunt, and I wanted to ensure that Hazel was her first victim. I took my time feeding. As I drank, I saw Anton for what he was: the zookeeper. It was his business to make sure his addicted crack users lived to see another day so they could return to purchase more drugs.

When I stepped outside, Rhymee looked feral because she was upset over me getting shot and her hunger consumed her.

"I am sorry. I did not mean to snap at you," I said softly, expecting her to be angry.

She stepped close to me and sniffed the air as I breathed, as if smelling a succulent roast, and then grabbed her stomach.

"Why can't I watch you feed?" she asked, sounding hurt.

"You can, but I wasn't prepared at that moment."

"Why?" she asked, not understanding.

"Would you mind if I suddenly had to watch you pee when you least expected it? Not that you have to anymore."

"Well, yes," she admitted.

"It is the same thing. Plus, I was trying to protect you. I did not want you to get shot."

"But it wouldn't kill me, right?" she asked, still not fully believing she was practically indestructible.

"No, but it itches," I said, tugging at my back. "I am having trouble reaching it."

Finally, I pulled a small bloody piece of metal, flattened on one side, from my wound. Abruptly it felt like a mound of worms were slithering in the gaping hole for a few seconds. Then I was healed.

I could tell Rhymee was in deep thought for a moment.

"Thad, I'm not mad," she said, gently kissing my cheek. "I understand, but you must do the same for me when it's time for me to feed. I don't want you to interfere no matter what, even if I'm attacked. What if we have to be apart? I need to be able to fend for myself."

She was right, but I hesitated to promise her. I knew I could not restrain myself if someone tried to harm her in any way, immortal or not.

"Well?"

"I just don't want to make a promise that I can't keep. I don't ever want to lie to you."

"Thad, you know me. If we were hunting four-leaf clovers and you found one first and offered it to me, what would I do?"

"You would keep hunting." I sighed.

"Correct! I would want to find my own luck, not have it handed to me. If you had brought me a pitcher of that drug lord's blood, I would've refused it. Please don't take this the wrong way because I'm pleased you are by my side helping me, but I need to handle Hazel on my own. Otherwise my hunger will not be satisfied."

I smiled. "Only my Rhymee would have a notion such as that one."

She took the slug from my hand. "If anyone knows what pain is, I do," she said, still trying to make her point.

"I will do my best to not interfere with your hunt, my lady, but that is all I can promise."

"Good enough," she responded, grabbing my hand. "What now?"

"Daybreak approaches. We need to stop for the night. We will pick up her trail again at dusk."

We found Hazel's trail at the bus station the next evening, and from there she was easy to follow. Bus eight had an antifreeze leak and had left a splotchy green liquid trail down the interstate.

Hazel was also traveling by night. I suppose she wanted to be alert at the same time we were.

Rhymee sprinted when she saw taillights. No one on the highway could see us because we were dressed in black. We moved as swiftly as a bird's shadow across the land.

"It's stopping," said Rhymee, pointing ahead.

Once we reached the bus stop, we remained in the distance.

"There she is, smoking a cigarette," said Rhymee contemptuously.

"Wait until she boards, and then we will follow," I instructed.

I shall never forget the look on Hazel's face when Rhymee boarded the bus. It was an expression of pure shock and terror.

She jumped up and was going to leave, but I motioned her to sit back down, threatening her with my eyes. At that late hour, there was only one other passenger on the bus, and he was sitting toward the front.

We casually walked to the back and sat down beside her.

Hazel puckered her brow and looked down.

"Do you remember me?" asked Rhymee.

"I never forget my targets," replied Hazel in a respectful tone.

"Why was I your target?" asked Rhymee curiously.

Hazel just sat there stubbornly.

"Why did you try to kill me?" asked Rhymee, growing impatient.

"You just sit there quietly and enjoy your ride because it is the last one you will ever take," I said, enjoying the threat.

"Bus dri—" Hazel tried to yell right before I grabbed her throat and hushed her.

"Make another sound, and you shall not leave the bus breathing," I whispered.

We had reached a part of Highway 40 where vast desert seemed to stretch out endlessly on either side with mountainous, cylindrical rock formations, rising up like skin irritations along the desert's surface.

"Rhymee, I will be back in a moment. Watch her," I advised.

Flashes of disgust and defiance radiated from Hazel's eyes as I walked up the aisle to the driver.

"We need off here," I casually requested.

"Sorry, sir, it's our policy to only stop at authorized locations," the driver answered without taking his eyes off the road.

"Look, I normally would not ask, but we have a sick one back there needing some fresh air. If you don't stop, you will have a pile of puke to clean up, and the other I fear," I said, exhaling near his face as I spoke. He would do as I requested after he took a few breaths.

"The other?" the driver asked.

"You know, diarrhea. She says it's going to start coming from both ends pretty soon."

"She better not, or she'll clean it up!" said the driver. "It'll make me puke too! I will stop the bus."

"The young girl is going to have to help me escort her."

I quickly made my way back down the aisle while the driver pulled over. I placed my hand over Hazel's mouth, and Rhymee gripped her wrist firmly as we led her off the bus.

Hazel gave the driver a pleading look, but he assumed it was due to her illness.

"Hope you feel better soon, ma'am," he offered, pulling the door open.

We stood quite a distance from the bus for fifteen minutes, expecting the driver to move on without us, but he didn't.

"Making a noise would be a horrible mistake," I said.

Hazel slightly nodded yes with watering eyes, so I carefully removed my hand. Her mouth was rash red from the shock I inflicted from touching her.

"Be back in a second," I told Rhymee.

I went to the bus and told the driver to go on without us.

"I can't do that. The desert goes on for miles," he said frustrated.

"We have family about fifty miles from here. I called them while she was over there puking. They will be here in less than an hour. They know this area well. I don't know if she will even be able to travel by then." I shrugged.

"I don't like this at all."

"Can we just move on, man? I have a schedule to keep!" fumed the only other passenger on the bus.

"Ay ay ay, I'm probably going to be written-up or fired over this," said the driver, shaking his head and pulling the door shut.

I raced back to Rhymee and scoped the area for a second.

"Up there!" I pointed to a large plateau rising about five hundred feet in the air.

We ran so fast Hazel's feet did not get the opportunity to touch the ground.

We reached the base.

"On the count of three?" I asked Rhymee, synchronizing our jump.

"We can't! We can't! We won't make it!" Hazel begged in disbelief.

Rhymee bent her knees to the same angle as mine, preparing herself for the jump.

"Three!" I shouted.

Hazel flew through the air alongside us, like a rock slung from a slingshot, screaming the entire time.

"Piece of cake," said Rhymee, landing with grace.

Hazel was wobbling, rubbing her wrists, and trying to get her bearings after we let her go.

"Now, why did you try to kill me?" asked Rhymee with a little more patience.

"You were just another job," spat Hazel.

Rhymee frowned, scratched her head, and then asked, "Who hired you?"

Hazel stubbornly did not answer.

"I can do many torturous things besides killing you, which would bring me a lot of pleasure, if you don't cooperate," threatened Rhymee in an emotionless voice.

"You wouldn't believe me even if I told you, you naive girl."

"Try me," said Rhymee.

I just sat down and listened since I had promised I would not interfere.

"If I tell you, will you let me go, let me live?" asked Hazel, trying to bargain.

"So you can continue to hunt and kill innocent people? Nothing you promise would make me believe you, you awful woman."

"I can change," she said innocently. "Give me a second chance."

"Then cooperate and tell me," demanded Rhymee.

Hazel thought she was making progress, so she began to talk.

"Creatures from the underworld hired me. I don't know much, but they appear to me in clouds of red mist. The one who speaks to me is called Lurhide, and her master is Salumus."

Rhymee glanced at me, losing focus of her interview.

"See, I told you that you wouldn't believe me."

"It is okay, Rhymee. Do you want me to take it from here?" I asked.

She shook her head no, so I remained quiet.

"Why do they want to kill me?" she asked.

"They really wanted to kill your entire family, but there was no opportunity, and you were the most special. I was ordered to focus on taking you out. There are a rare few like you scattered across the world. I was ordered to help exterminate you and your family in exchange for immortality, but I failed," said Hazel, choking up for the first time.

"Others where?"

"I can't say, but I now believe they are powerless unless they get the help of humans. I realize they lied to me about everything. They used me."

"Thad, I need to speak with you for a moment," said Rhymee, turning her attention to me and pulling me away from Hazel's range of hearing.

"What is it?" I asked concerned.

"I can't do this. I can't kill her. Can't we drop her off at the nearest police station or something?" she asked.

"Uh, no! They would think we were crazy and end up arresting us instead of her! Rhymee, you need to eat! Are you not crazed by hunger?"

"Yes, very much so. It's just that I…I don't know if I can live with that decision. What if she really can change?"

I knew what I had to do, but it was going to be hard.

"I understand," I sympathized. "I tell you what. I will leave you up here for a moment alone with her so you can talk a little more before you make your final decision."

"Okay, but what will we do with her if I decide to let her go?"

"She can hitchhike for all I care. I am sure she is used to that," I pointed out coldly.

"I won't be too long," said Rhymee.

I leapt down from the plateau.

Around fifteen minutes later, I heard a thud and a loud cry. I gave Rhymee her privacy until I could stand it no more. I leaped back up on the plateau to find her standing over Hazel's body. She yet again stabbed Rhymee in the back; only this time Rhymee took a double hit.

I had known the heartless crone carried her weapons and, in my absence, she would use them given the chance. She had no respect for Rhymee, still seeing her as the weak girl she had attacked before.

That was all it took for Rhymee to lose her compassion and control. Hazel screamed for only a second before becoming Rhymee's first meal as a vampire.

I inspected Rhymee's back. "Hold still," I said. "I am going to pull the knives out."

Rhymee nodded.

I pulled quickly, and the wounds sealed shut. She winced but made no noise.

"Are you okay?"

"It's too late now, even if I'm not," said Rhymee quietly.

I could not find the words to comfort her. "Rhymee, I do not know what I can—"

"I don't blame you, Thad, and I knew how this hunt would end. It's just I know that I've lost a piece of my innocence I can never regain. I just…my father would be ashamed of me."

"I know how you feel. Although I lost my father many years ago, I would have trouble explaining what I am to him as well," I empathized.

"I just need some time to think. I've been on the move since my change. I haven't had an opportunity to really think about anything other than hunger."

"You shall be given the time. Even if I need to leave you alone for a while, I will understand. Now, promise me you will wait here," I requested, lifting Hazel's body.

"Where are you going?" she asked timidly.

"To take care of her. I don't want to leave her for the buzzards," I said.

"Shouldn't I take care of her since I created the mess?" asked Rhymee.

"Come on then. You can watch."

I sprinted with the corpse draped across my shoulder for about a mile until we found a good spot to bury her.

I dug fast like a mole deep into the ground. I then tossed her in, along with her knives and purse, and covered her back up.

"Do you want to say something?"

Rhymee thought for a moment and then said, "Understand, Hazel, I'm only the deliverer, not the judge of you because I did not bear your burdens. I hope you find peace in death. Your turn," she said with sincerity, expecting me to speak as well.

I stood over her grave and said the only thing I could think of that I truly meant.

"The dead know nothing, and that is best for you, so you cannot hurt anyone else."

I noticed my words kind of cheered Rhymee up, and she halfway smiled.

I walked over and picked up a misshapen boulder, which a normal man could never lift without the help of a bulldozer, and I dropped it right on top of Hazel.

"Headstone," I simply said.

Rhymee lifted an eyebrow and then said, "Well, one thing is for certain: no one will ever find her."

"Are you ready to go?" I asked.

"Most definitely. I want to go home."

"Lead the way, you tracking fiend," I teased, trying to lighten her mood even further.

"Thad, we can spend the day in Albuquerque and then make haste from there," said Rhymee, running ahead of me. "Are you coming?"

"Right away, my dear," I called out, enjoying her scent as I followed.

A VAMPIRE'S SCENT

We traveled swiftly until we reached the long, winding dirt road leading to the farm known as Kettle Springs Road. The road had a natural spring that welled up. Its overflow fell into a cast-iron pot about a half mile down the lane.

The oak trees on each side of the road were so thick and ancient that their canopies interlocked and formed a natural roof.

Rhymee's sprint changed to a jog, then to a fast walk, and then she stopped.

"What is it?" I asked.

"I am surprised by how well I can see through the darkness. Now I know why my family, for as far back as I can remember, has called this road Spider Lane. I've never seen so many webs and spiders in my entire life. It's as if they are taking over, and I hate them," she said.

"They are always here in these numbers during this time of year," I explained, pulling a hairy, plump spider from its web. It tried biting me. I let it crawl on my hand a moment then carefully put it back.

She looked up at the hundreds of webs shaking and swaying in the slight breeze. "It's as if we've entered a giant funnel web. I keep imagining the mother of them all jumping out on us."

"You're a vampire. I'm sure you could take it."

She suddenly looked at me, half smiling.

"If they attack, will you rescue me?" she asked, full of orneriness.

I walked over close to her.

"I would give my life for you," I whispered, and I kissed her cheek.

"And I for you," she said, hugging me tightly for a moment. "But we're already dead!"

"Funny, Rhymee. You know what I meant. I would become completely obliterated for you."

She wove around and ducked under the newly strung webs so the sticky, silken strings would not cling to her face and clothing. "This trip's been long. I can't wait to see my family."

She picked up her pace once we reached a neighbor's open cow pasture. We were about two miles from her parents' farm.

I suddenly caught a strange scent in the air. "Rhymee, wait! Do you smell something odd?"

She stopped and took a deep breath. "Yes, I smell it too, but I can't tell what it is." She studied my face and noticed my grim expression. "Is it dangerous?"

I grabbed her hand and led her to a thicket. "It is."

"What is it, Thad?"

"Another vampire, one I do not recognize, has been through here.

"But they don't feed on the innocent, right?" she asked, her eyes glowing widely with trepidation.

"They are not supposed to, but more vampires have come into existence without the council's approval. They do not understand our ways. They do not hold our morals."

"We have to hurry!" said Rhymee, rushing ahead and ignoring my request to wait.

"Rhymee, they are dangerous killers." I shouted.

"If my family's been hurt, I swear I'll kill whoever is responsible."

"And I shall help you, but we must proceed with caution."

We darted from tree to tree until the house came into view. There was a light on in the living room, and we could hear an old Western playing on the TV, but no one stirred inside the house. However, no noise was to be expected at 2:00 a.m. on a Friday night.

"Listen quietly, and you can hear each of them breathing," I suggested.

Rhymee listened intently and then smiled. "I can hear Dad snoring. They're okay."

"Rhymee, please wait here," I urged, wanting to search the area a little longer to make sure the strange vampire was not lingering around the place.

"What are you going to do?" asked Rhymee curiously.

"I am going to make sure that the threat is gone and that your family is safe." I replied. I loved her family.

"I'll go with you," she offered. "Now that I know they're safe, I'll help."

"It is best if I check things out alone. Except for Frost and Egan, no other vampire knows you are changed, and this vampire is strange to me and could be dangerous. It could turn into a nasty confrontation. If I need you, I will call to you," I promised, giving her a hug and kiss.

"All right, but if I hear trouble, I'm coming to you."

"Good enough."

I followed the vampire's scent. It had been a female, and she had lingered and slept against the same rock Rhymee had often rested on during our many conversations we had had through the years. She left just hours before our return. "What does she want?" I asked aloud. As far as I knew, it was the first time a vampire other than me had ever passed through this area. I felt uneasy. I did not want to leave her parents and sisters unprotected, but I had no choice. It was too dangerous for

Rhymee to stay. Even if her parents did not catch sight of her, someone else that knew her might. *The threat is gone*, I called to Rhymee. I was standing near the barn when she came and joined me.

"Thad, now that this has happened, I don't know if I can bear leaving them," she said, giving me a worried look.

"Too many people know who you are. That's why we had to go through the trouble of faking your death and terrorizing Mr. Jenkins. I wish we could stay, Rhymee. This place is just as much my home now as it is yours." I sighed.

"I know…I know…I just..." Rhymee began to choke up. "Thad, I would never forgive myself if something happened to them that I could've stopped."

"I couldn't either, Rhymee. I want to make sure they are safe too. I can do something to deter other vampires from coming here by placing a warning that this territory is off limits. If this vampire ever tries to pass through again, she will see the sign and know to stay away."

"That makes me feel better. What will you do to warn her? What type of sign?"

"It is a simple line with a dot at each end, one above and one below. I will carve the markings in numerous places. Other vampires will know what it means, especially with our scent in the area."

"I wouldn't know what it means," Rhymee pointed out. "What if it's a vampire that's been turned without the council's permission?"

"But you soon will. It is my duty to teach you our language. Rhymee, those rogue vampires will not be around much longer. They are being hunted down and destroyed. "

"Wow." Rhymee became quiet as she starred at the ground. "Won't the rain wash our scent away?"

"No. Magical traces cannot be washed away by weather."

"Oh. How long will it take to post these warnings?"

"At most, a few days."

"When you finish, I'll be ready to go with you, but where will we stay in the meantime?"

"The forest would be the most secluded and a good place to teach you some defensive moves."

Rhymee lifted an eyebrow. "Why?"

"Because next time you hunt, I don't what you to get stabbed if it can be prevented."

"I feel like I'm a nuisance. Look at all the stuff you've had to help me with in the last few days."

I laughed hard at her comment. "I enjoy every second with you—always have."

"I hope you still feel that way in fifty years."

"You are going to have to start thinking in longer terms," I said, pressing her head to my chest.

We sat against the trunk of a tree, holding each other through the night. At daybreak, I began the work of posting signs around the perimeter of the farm while Rhymee listened to her family from the cover of the trees. Sorrow etched her face. As she watched, she hid her emotions from me. I could have finished the signs in a day, but I knew she needed longer than that. I suspected seeing her family grieve prolonged her misery and made matters worse. Was a couple days enough time? Was it wrong to ask her to leave? Could I make her happy and fill the void where her family once was? I hoped this was not another mistake that I could throw on the massive pile of the many I had already made with her.

SAYING MY GOOD-BYES

In the days before we left the farm, I had constant mood swings. I knew my life was rapidly changing. I was overjoyed to be alive, immortal, and getting to travel to different parts of the world and saddened by the fact I had to leave home and hunt to survive. I was worried about leaving my family unprotected. The unfamiliar vampire hadn't been back, but that didn't give me confidence. Would my parents and sisters be okay? Could they continue to run the farm without my help?

While watching and listening, I noticed my sisters eagerly helping with the household chores. They washed dishes without being asked. Rhondel started doing the laundry while Rhegan dusted and tidied things in the living room, bathroom, and bedrooms. I was proud of them for wanting to take care of my parents.

Dad was completely wrapped up in trying to find out who had broken in the house and attacked me. He took a part of their savings and hired a private investigator. The man was at the house several hours inspecting where Hazel had entered, where they found me on the floor, and at one point, he started walking to right where I was hiding. I had to quickly move to a different spot.

Later that same day, salesmen arrived, and my dad entered into a two-year contract and bought a top of the line alarm system.

When my mom could, she stayed to herself and was mostly quiet. She seemed to come out of her daze just long enough to cook or do the things she could not ignore. I could hear her sniffle occasionally, which made it hard for me to suppress my own tears.

That night, when the house became quiet, I heard them all go into a separate room. Rhondel went into my old bedroom while Rhegan went to theirs. Mom stayed in the kitchen after dinner, and Dad went to the living room. Except for Rhegan, they each started crying. Dad turned on the TV and was watching the news to cover the noise of his tears.

Rhondel bawled the hardest. "Dad will find her, Rhymee. I swear it, and if he doesn't, I will, even if it takes me a lifetime." It took all my strength not to go to her and show her that I was still here with them. I grabbed my stomach and pushed on the knots forming inside.

I knew my mom could hear Rhondel when she stopped rinsing a dish to listen. She walked over to the paper towel rack, tore one off, and blew her nose. She didn't rush to comfort Rhondel, maybe because she didn't have the strength to.

Rhegan went upstairs and got in bed. "Rhymee, I know you are out there somewhere, and I'll get to see you again. I love you and goodnight."

I'd listened to all I could stand. I ran deep into the forest, stopped, and began crying. I couldn't suppress it any more. I was in ruins. Green orbs the size of tennis balls began to hover and circle around me in the night air, like bubbles swirling inside a lava lamp. My fangs fell to my lower lip, but I didn't care. I was a monster of the worst kind. *How could I allow my family to suffer like this?* I leaned my head against the bark of a pine tree.

I suddenly felt Thad's hand on my shoulder. I hesitated to turn and look at him. I was a mess and was trying hard not to snuffle.

"Rhymee, please look at me," he gently asked.

"I'm sorry. I don't want you seeing me like this."

He grabbed my hair, gently twisted it, and lifted it over my shoulder. Then he kissed the back of my neck.

I couldn't resist him. When I turned, I noticed soft light coating his eyes. A few of his blue tears occasionally bumped into and followed mine as they slowly rose to the starry sky.

"Rhymee, please stop crying. I think I know a way to help you and your family cope with this sorrow."

"How?" I was very skeptical.

"You can speak to your family through hypnosis, but you must be careful of what you say. You cannot let them know you have become a vampire, even in their dreams."

"What do I do?"

"After Rhondel goes to bed, you can start with your sisters, but they must be fast asleep. The new alarm system poses a problem. You will need to gain entrance to the house without setting it off, but I think I know a possible solution."

"What?"

"Your dad has a habit of stepping out on the porch each night before he locks the front door. While he is out there, fill your breath with your intentions, and then whisper to him from the edge of the woods. Exhale deeply into the night air, casting your breath in his direction. Tell him not to lock the front door or to set the alarm. If he has heard you, we will soon know."

"Have you done this before?"

"Many times. The ability comes in useful from time to time, especially when hunting."

"Will you come with me?"

"If you wish. Once you are inside your sisters' bedroom, fill it with your breath. Then you can sneak over to each one and tell them what you want."

"I don't know what I'd say."

"When the time comes, you will. Do you want to try?"

I nodded. "I think it'll help."

"Let's go. We do not want to miss your dad. When we draw near, we both need to put our sunglasses on. We don't want him spotting our glowing eyes through the darkness," suggested Thad, grabbing my hand.

When we reached the tree line, we put our glasses on and crawled underneath the base of a large cedar tree.

"I have watched you often from this very spot," admitted Thad.

I hugged him tightly as we waited. About an hour had passed when my dad came out. He didn't just stand on the porch; he walked out in the yard and looked up to the sky.

"Now is your chance," Thad urged.

I crawled from under the tree and stood behind it.

"Don't set the alarm or lock the doors," I whispered over and over again, casting my breath in his direction, and then I waited.

My dad looked around as if he had heard something.

I quickly ducked. Had he seen me? A part of me wanted him to.

He stood there a moment longer, peering into the shadows, and then he slowly made his way back to the house. After he stepped inside, I listened for the sound of the locking mechanism inside the door handle. I smiled in relief when I realized he had heard and listened to me. The door remained unlocked and the alarm was still deactivated.

"Good job, Rhymee," said Thad, crawling from under the tree. "Now, we must wait until they are all asleep."

"Rhondel, it's past your bedtime," I heard Dad say.

"Yes, sir," she answered, climbing the stairs.

I could hear Mom set a glass of water on her night stand, fluff her pillow, and pull the sheets back before getting into bed. Dad soon joined her, and before long, I could hear him snoring.

"Are you ready?" asked Thad.

"As I ever will be."

Thad and I leapt across the yard, quietly stepped on the porch, opened the front door with care, and crept up the stairs. Before entering my sisters' bedroom, I stopped and calmed my nerves. I knew this creaky door well. I grabbed the white rusted knob and cautiously turned it in small measured degrees then slowly pushed the door open just enough for the two of us to squeeze through. While wishing for them both to remain asleep, I took another deep breath then breathed out. I looked back at Thad reluctantly. He smiled and motioned for me to go on.

If I whisper to them, will it wake them up?

No, he answered.

I went to Rhondel's bed first and knelt down on the floor beside her. "You've always been strong. Take care of Mom, Dad, and Rhegan. You don't need to worry about finding my attacker, she's dead. I can't tell you how or why, but you must know that I'm okay. Don't mourn over me another second. You swear?" I noticed Rhondel nod in her sleep. I paused to think for a moment. All the dangers my family had recently encountered came to mind: Hazel, the mercurides, and the mysterious vampire that had passed through. I wanted to make sure Rhondel and Rhegan weren't helpless. "I want you to have my bow, and I want Rhegan to have my throwing knives. Promise me that you'll practice until you become very skilled with it. Help Rhegan practice and read a story to her before bed."

"I promise," Rhondel muttered. I drew back and looked over at Thad. He was leaned against a wall.

Did I wake her?

She still sleeps.

I again filled the room with my breath for good measure. Then I painstakingly crawled over to Rhegan. "You were right. I'm fine. Never think otherwise. First thing in the morning, I want you to go get my throwing knives from my room. I'm giving them to you. Listen to Rhondel and follow her instructions."

I stood up and headed toward the door. I stopped and turned to look at them one last time. "If there is ever any danger, run and hide first before you resort to using your weapons. Take care of each other and Mom and Dad. I love you both very much."

I was more wary of entering my parents' room. Their door was newer and not noisy, but I knew both of them were light sleepers.

Instead of speaking to them separately, I talked to them together. "I'm watching you guys, and it's tearing me up to see the two of you so sad. I'm in a better place, a place where I don't get cold or feel pain. Please don't grieve over me any longer. I know not much time has passed since you had to let me go, but Rhondel and Rhegan need you. Both of you were right in getting an alarm system. Don't ever let your guard down. Dad, don't waste any more money trying to find my killer. She's been punished and is dead. I love you both so much, and I promise I will come back to check on you from time to time."

I motioned to Thad that I was finished, and we left the house swiftly without making a sound.

We walked back to the dense cedar tree and waited there. The distant sky grew to a dark shade of pink. "Would you like to stay somewhere secluded while I finish marking the area?"

"That'd be nice," I said, not realizing what he had in mind.

"If you like, you can stay in the well. It is close to your family yet concealed. You can hear them nicely from there."

"No, thank you! There's no way I'm going down in that hole." I shivered. "The thought of it gives me the creeps. I don't know how you stood it. Besides, I'm claustrophobic."

"You never know. You might like it."

"I'm certain I won't," I said. "I'll just wait here for you."

Thad laughed. "Okay, the cedar tree will work. We should probably head out tomorrow night," he said.

I nodded, frowning slightly. The time with my family had gone by too quickly.

"If you want, we will stay longer. I want you to be happy."

"No. I'm fine. I want to go with you. I'll see you later."

"I love you, Rhymee. You have made me happy, more than I ever thought possible," he said.

"I love you too, Thad."

"Tonight, if you are up to it, I would like to show you what you are capable of."

"Okay, that sounds fun." I forced a smile.

Later that Sunday morning, my family woke in better spirits. Rhondel and Rhegan ran into each other in my room, retrieving the bow and knives I had given them.

"What are you doing in here?" asked Rhondel.

"Rhymee told me I could have her knives," answered Rhegan.

"Did you hear her in the night?"

"Yep, and as much as I don't want to, she told me to listen to you."

"Come on," ordered Rhondel, grabbing my old bow.

"Where we goin'?" asked Rhegan.

"To practice, like I promised."

"Rhondel, don't tell Mom and Dad this, but I think Rhymee's alive."

"Me too. I won't tell."

After hearing my sisters' discussion, I found myself chuckling. I had to admit, I felt better. Mom and Dad did not talk about my visit, but I could tell their moods had changed somewhat. Mom seemed to bustle around the house with renewed hope while Dad made coffee for himself before going to the garage to work on Old Green.

As I enjoyed listening to my family, the day seemed to go by quickly. Before I expected, Thad returned to me.

"The markings are finished. If she ever passes this way again, she will know to turn around and stay away," he explained, seeming satisfied with his work. "It will be dusk before too long. Are you ready to train?"

"Yes," I said eagerly, jumping up.

That night, Thad and I spent our time exploring the mountainous terrain together. At first, I lacked confidence in everything he wanted me to attempt. My body felt energetic, like it could never tire, but I didn't feel indestructible.

"It's interesting to watch you race across the countryside with ease." I stopped to laugh a moment at my new ability, and he laughed with me.

"Do you feel invincible yet?"

I ran ahead of him.

"I can't describe it. I feel like the ground is a giant trampoline that I can't get hurt on." I shouted.

"Running with you is the most fun I have ever had!" he yelled.

"Good! Then we will do a lot more of it!"

When it came time to leap down from extreme heights, I didn't trust that I could. I'd always been afraid of heights.

Thad constantly reassured me. "Rhymee, you cannot hurt yourself. Remember how quickly you recovered after being stabbed? Remember how you gracefully bounded to the window at the hospital? The magic within you recognizes gravity, but it is not bound by it. That's why you can leap great distances."

"I know. I just need to get used to this," I said. "What if I land wrong and break something?"

"Come over here for a moment, please," he requested. He was standing under an old, gnarled tree full of thick branches. "Okay, normally this would rip your flesh open, wouldn't it?" he asked, placing his hand against the bark. Using it like sandpaper, he began rubbing his palm up and down, deliberately trying to cut himself.

"Yes."

"Look," he said, dusting the particles of bark away to show there was no scrapes or cuts. "You try."

I walked over and rubbed my hand lightly on the tree, and when that didn't hurt, I rubbed harder.

"See," he said. "And if you ever fall, I will be there to catch you."

"Really…so if I climb this tree, you will catch me when I jump?"

"Yes, but you must leap up there, not climb. Deal?"

I smiled, sized up the tree, and jumped to a high branch. For a moment, I looked at the canopy that stretched for miles around me and took a breath of the juniper scented air. I leaped to another branch that I thought would support my weight, but it instantly snapped. I could have caught another one, but I deliberately didn't. *I trust him*, I thought as I freefell.

"Got you," he said, catching me and holding me close to his chest. "Want to try again?"

"If this is the outcome each time, then yes."

He laughed and kissed me on my forehead. "If you try jumping from that branch right there, I shall carry you through the forest on top of my shoulders," he promised, pointing to the thickest, highest limb he could find.

"Like a piggyback ride?"

"Yep…you have just got to make that one jump on your own."

I didn't say a word. I quickly leapt to the top of the tree, enjoyed the scenery for just a second longer, and then glided down. My mind was on Thad.

"You didn't seem to have any trouble."

"No, I think I can do that from now on. Okay, where are we going?"

"Where would you like to go, my lady?" he asked.

"Anywhere with you is fine," I said.

"Climb aboard," he requested.

I did as he said, but I suddenly felt shy. I held back laughter from the awkward ride, but I didn't want to get down either.

"Rhymee, are you okay with leaving?" he asked, pressing forward through the undergrowth.

"I'm just anxious. I'm also worried that the strange vampire will come back," I admitted.

"I could be wrong, but sometimes vampires track each other out of curiosity or loneliness. I really feel if that vampire had been hunting, one of your family members or neighbors would have come up missing."

"You're right. It's just scary leaving home for the first time. I'm sure I will have fun once I take that first step. Why have you slowed down?" I asked.

"Because we are here. Do you trust me?" he asked. He walked a little farther up the hill he had been steadily climbing.

"Of course. Why?" I asked.

"Hang on! I need to get a run at this."

"What are we—" I choked his neck. We were freefalling from the top of a sheer cliff. I couldn't help but scream.

"It's okay. I've got you!" he shouted through the air.

Our land was surprisingly soft. "Can we do that again?"

"As many times as you would like, but look, this is why I brought you here," he said.

I had not been paying attention. We were standing directly in front of a waterfall. It was beautiful. The clear, pure water plummeted down the gray limestone overhang that Thad had dove from a few minutes earlier. The center of the waterfall was solid rock, but wild ferns and globe willows grew in abundance on each side. The water basin was comprised of white and pink flint stone and surrounded by cattails and reeds.

"What a magical place!" I exclaimed.

"I have passed through here before. I thought you might like it."

"I love it. It's as if someone built this place and planted this foliage deliberately."

We sat beneath the fall, listening to the water and talking until the following evening.

I was scared of but also looking forward to my future with Thad. I told myself it was time to grow up and to accept my fate. Things had happened beyond my control to throw me into becoming a vampire. What was I to do—cower down and hide from the world? It wasn't in my nature. The magic within me was a gift, and I intended to use it to the world's advantage.

FOREWARNINGS

The air was thick with low-lying fog as we prepared to leave. Again, Rhymee had told her dad to leave the alarm off and the door unlocked.

"When can we come back to check on them," asked Rhymee.

"When would you like to return?"

"Is six months too soon?"

"No, but we will need to take care that no one sees you," I said as we crept to her room.

I sat on the bed, stared out the window, and listened while Rhymee gathered her things. "Remember, only a backpack full of clothes. Anything heavier will become a nuisance."

"Already taken care of," Rhymee said, twirling around with her blue backpack strapped to her shoulders.

She said her final good-byes silently from the front yard, and then we slowly headed through the forest. Our plan was to visit Egan's house for a while and then continue on to Europe.

Rhymee suddenly stopped and searched the area; then I picked up the familiar scent.

"Sighka, we know you are here. Show yourself," I groaned. A large brown hoot owl swooped down in front of us. "What do you want?" I asked.

"Now, now. Patience is a virtue," said the fairy, changing form.

Rhymee grinned and cut her eyes to me.

"You barely caught us. We were just heading out on a long journey," I pointed out.

"I caught you at exactly the time I wanted to, Thadacus Goodridge," she said in her light, airy voice.

"And?"

"I think I will accompany the two of you."

"Why?" asked Rhymee.

"Rhymee, I want to help you."

"What? I don't understand."

"She has no need of your services," I said.

"Oh, but she will!"

"What nonsense do you speak of?" I asked.

"For one, the rogues are multiplying. There are now thirty-nine."

"Thirty-nine?" I was shocked by the rising number.

"That is not the worst of it. The mercurides were released. They have crossed the gate back into Lethun," reported Sighka.

"Why is that bad? I say good riddance!"

"I agree," said Rhymee. "It's a relief knowing they won't be hanging around here anymore."

"My people can only control who exits Argent, not who enters. Some of us feel Salumus and his band will return with new bodies and with more followers."

"How is that possible?" asked Rhymee.

"The creatures of Lethun do not die as we do. A vampire's magic comes from that world. That is why you are now immortal. It is a long story. I will fill you in along the way," explained the fairy, assuming she was going with us.

"Why would they return after the tortures they endured?" I asked, skeptical of Sighka's theories.

"Vengeance and a thirst for power, of course."

"Why do you want to help me?" asked Rhymee.

I knew why, but I did not want anyone to know, including Rhymee, for her own protection.

"Sighka!" I slightly shook my head, indicating I disagreed with her sharing what she had told me at the hospital the night Rhymee was dying.

"It is necessary," she said in a serious tone, looking at me gravely for the first time since I had met her.

"I must train you to your fullest abilities, and only my kind knows how to show you the secrets earth holds. Understand I take a great risk in coming. My people are slowly dividing. Some would see you destroyed because of your abilities."

"What abilities? I'm just like any other vampire, aren't I?" Rhymee asked, turning to me.

"No, you are not just like any other vampire," I said softly.

"Why?"

"You carry the blood of earth's warriors. It is in your nature to destroy any threat to this world," Sighka said. "Your ancestors killed the mercurides. That is why they watched and had a killer stalk you and your family. They were trying to kill others as well."

"Earth's warriors? What are those?" asked Rhymee.

"You and your family are descendants of the Gauls, and the Gauls are sacred to the fairies," I explained.

"The mercurides were especially interested in me? Why?"

"I have never seen another human like you. You are quite different, seeing beyond what others can. You have always known and accepted earth as a magical place. Its secrets are locked away in your mind. Over the years, you have suppressed much of what you once accepted as fact. I can help you remember. Do not come down hard on yourself for being vampire. I truly believe it was your destiny," said the fairy. "I will give you a small example. What did you once think of the moon?"

"The both of you would think I'm crazy. It was just my vivid imagination as a small child," said Rhymee, doubting herself.

"Tell us, for you are not wrong," coaxed Sighka.

"Fine, but I don't believe it now," said Rhymee.

"I could never think you are crazy. Go on," I said.

Rhymee sighed before beginning. "I used to dream the moon, at its fullest, had the power to wake suppressed dreams, ambitions, and thoughts. See! I told you I'm crazy!"

"Many great thoughts and ideas came to life on such nights. If a people had a united cause to fight and the battle was fought under such a light, those people would always come out the victor. So see, Rhymee, you are correct. You should let your instincts guide you more," encouraged Sighka.

I was amazed, and at that moment, all I could think of was Rhymee as a small child dancing under the moon. I then understood why it was so special to her and why she wanted me to see it on the night I first met her so long ago.

"Thad, she should come. I want to learn more. She's done nothing but help us," said Rhymee.

"Why can't we wait and see how things turn out? The mercurides may never return for all we know."

"If they do return, we will have no time," said Sighka. "Make no mistake, she needs to have use of her powers. If your kind, whether it be the rogues or the others when they find out, does not kill her, the mercurides will do their best upon their return. A war is imminent."

I could not tell Rhymee no.

"Can you keep up, fairy?" I asked, taking the lead at a sprint.

She laughed and quickly changed back into the hoot owl and took flight.

Sighka's news terrified me. I knew it would do no good to worry about things beyond my control, so I decided to focus on our current situation and remain happy while the opportunity lasted.

Heading south, we nimbly ran through the forest, making our way toward Louisiana and Egan's former house. Sighka soared from above, sometimes appearing like a tiny, brown speck against the round, bright moon. Holding out my hand, I turned around and glanced at Rhymee. She didn't hesitate to grab it, and she smiled excitedly as we continued to run. I didn't know what trials lay ahead of us, but we were together. That was all that mattered.